MAHALA

MAHALA

Carol Marques Barrios

Arcade Publishing · New York

Arcade Publishing books may be purchased in bulk at special discounts for sales promotion, corporate gifts, fund-raising, or educational purposes. Special editions can also be created to specifications. For details, contact the Special Sales Department, Arcade Publishing, 307 5th Avenue, 4th Floor, New York, NY 10016 or arcade@skyhorsepublishing.com.

Arcade Publishing® is a registered trademark of Skyhorse Publishing, Inc.®, a Delaware corporation.

Visit our website at www.arcadepub.com.

10 9 8 7 6 5 4 3 2 1

Library of Congress Cataloging-in-Publication Data is available on file.

Cover design by Heather VenHuizen
Cover photos from Shutterstock

Print ISBN: 978-1-64821-206-2
Ebook ISBN: 978-1-64821-210-9

Printed in the United States of America

For my father Erwin S. Marques.

Thank you to my husband Al (George) and my daughters Alayna, Katrina, and Celia for believing in me when I said I was going to write this novel. I love you more than you could ever fathom. I couldn't have done this without your loving support.

Thank you to my editor, Ellen Coughtrey, whose guidance on the story's pacing and physicality encouraged me to write a beautiful novel that I am immensely proud of.

PROLOGUE

1898—St. Vincent, British West Indies

JOHN SIMONS SAW THE CLOUDS first, filling the sky over the southern windward coast of the island. The boiling house where he and Ganesh Patandine supervised the laborers as they milled raw cane into sugar always emitted large clouds of steam, but these were different—dark and strange. One by one, the men paused and watched, distracted, when suddenly the air around them grew intensely hot, whipping hot ash and rocks across the plantation.

A quarter mile away from the boiling house, Emily ran across the yard in search of her mother, stumbling through the debris falling around her, as fast as her toddler legs could carry her. She found her hanging laundry and chatting with her best friend, Kavita. "Clouds—big clouds coming! Mama, do you see them, too?" Emily yelled at the top of her little lungs. Jane scooped her up into her arms. "Sweetling, come to Mama. There is no need to worry. I'm sure everything will be okay." Kavita helped Jane quickly gather her laundry back into the basket so it wouldn't be marred by what looked like ash floating down from the dark clouds looming above them. The two women ran inside Jane's house to find the rest of Jane's children and make sure they were safe.

Large clumps of ash fell from the dark sky as the plantation grew frenetic with activity. Workers rushed about looking for their loved ones, making sure they were safe. *Soufrière*, they whispered fearfully. Although the inhabitants of the island had never witnessed an eruption, they knew the famed story of almost ninety years ago when Soufrière—St. Vincent's only active volcano—violently exploded in a cascade of lava and destruction in the northern part of the island. The clouds of smoke and ash were visible over the eighteen-mile stretch of the small Caribbean island. Ganesh and John quickly maneuvered through the mill area, trying to ensure the safety of the workers as well as the security of the mill house itself. Small rocks and debris pelted the yard. The intensity of the windstorm's heat increased.

"We need to get inside. Now!" Ganesh yelled.

"We need to get the others to safety first," replied John.

Just then Ankit ran in front of them, screaming in pain. "My eyes! They're burning up! I can't see! Help me!" Both Ganesh and John rushed over. Ganesh grabbed a wooden water bucket and threw its contents into Ankit's face to flush the smoking ash from his eyes. John pulled a rag from his back pocket and dipped it in a second water bucket close by, then placed it over the young man's eyes to soothe the pain. "It's going to be okay, Ankit, just stay still and try to remain calm."

"I'll stay with him if you go check on our families. Take something to protect yourself in case the debris starts to swirl again," said Ganesh.

"The wind is starting to subside a bit. If I'm quick I should be able to make it," replied John. He grabbed a wood plank from the scrap pile to hold over his head as a shield as he left.

John made it home to the women and children without injury. He found his wife Jane and her friend Kavita soothing and reassuring one of his daughters. Jane had Emily wrapped in a protective embrace. He scanned the room for the rest of his brood and came up empty. "Where are the boys and Elizabeth?"

"Henry and Rudolph took Elizabeth in the next room to read to her. They thought that would calm her down," answered Jane.

"I'm so relieved that you are okay, my love. I don't know what I would have done if I didn't find my precious family safe," John murmured. "Ganesh and I have had reports from messengers from the North some months ago of some unusual vibration. It might be that that was a precursor to this eruption."

Two days later, ash still dropped from the sky. Plantation workers closest to Soufrière had evacuated. Despite the dense rainforest and mountainous terrain, the smoking eruption was visible from all points of the island. Sugar mills and homes collapsed from the volcano's intense tremors; over 1,600 people lost their lives in the ensuing destruction. People on the leeward side were able to evacuate by sea due to the passenger canoe services between Chateaubelair and Kingstown, the capital, but the windward side did not have the safety of protected harbors—and consequently saw many more die.

Soufrière continued to erupt for the better part of a year—in May, as well as September, October, and the following March. The neighbors grew used to the constant evacuation and safety procedures; the children returned to playing in the communal yard; and Kavita, despite the ever-present danger, found herself once more longing for a baby of her own.

CHAPTER I

Kavita

1899—St. Vincent, British West Indies

KAVITA PATANDINE LAY DOUBLED OVER on her kitchen floor. The pain was immense, gripping her lower abdomen—a familiar yet dreaded sensation that she knew all too well.

She'd collapsed shortly after her husband had lovingly kissed her on the cheek and bid her farewell for the day. She knew it wouldn't be long before her best friend would stop by for their daily ritual of pleasantly exchanging the details of their lives over steaming cups of masala chai, as they had done over the past ten years. Kavita gritted her teeth as the cramps worsened. Her sweat began to drench her clothes, but still, she could not move.

"Please Jane . . . come," Kavita prayed.

She thought back to when she and Ganesh had first arrived in St. Vincent from India. It was a new start for them, a chance to escape the poverty they had experienced in their home village. Ganesh had agreed to enter a seven-year indenture for a sugar mill and was promised opportunities for advancement after the contract was fulfilled.

Shortly after they arrived, Kavita was convinced they had made a catastrophic mistake. She was homesick for her family and her village. She desperately missed her parents, grandparents, and siblings, and the house they all shared. She had grown up extremely close to her family and although they had little money, they took great pride in their integrity and honor above all else. They were a family filled with rich cultural traditions that celebrated a long-established way of life. Kavita accepted these values, as did her husband.

She remembered being both nervous and excited to be married to Ganesh when she was just a teenage girl. Their families had known each other for years, promising their children to each other at birth. Her parents and grandparents and their parents before them had had similar arrangements. Neither Kavita nor Ganesh ever questioned that this was their destiny.

What she hadn't counted on was moving to a distant place that was separated from her family home by two vast oceans that took more than three months to cross. The homesickness had lessened over time. She found that adhering to her cultural Indian traditions helped her feel connected to her family in this faraway place.

The door creaked open. Jane shrieked. "Kavi—what on earth has happened? Beti, can you hear me? Kavita!"

"Jane, I knew you would come." She opened her eyes slightly. "It's happening again."

Kavita felt Jane's arms around her as she dragged her up onto the kitchen chair.

"It's just like the other times." Kavita murmured, staring down at the blood on the floor.

"Maybe it's not the end this time. Maybe it's something that can be stopped since it's so early," Jane reassured her.

"I pray," she replied, wincing at another wave of cramps. "From your mouth to Parvati's ears. Let her make this right for me and Ganesh." Tears prickled in her eyes.

Jane started toward the door to get the doctor.

"Wait. Don't leave me. I'm scared." Kavita began to shiver.

"You're going to be okay," Jane rubbed her friend's back gently.

"I—I've—failed him again," she sobbed.

"Nonsense, Kavi, he loves you. We'll pray harder together," Jane soothed her. "Let me just get the doctor for you. I'll be right back, I promise." Jane looked at her pleadingly.

Finally, Kavita let Jane's hand slip out of her grip. A sob escaped her lips as she watched Jane dash out her front door.

Two weeks after Jane had rescued her off her kitchen floor, Kavita was still barely able to drag herself out of bed each morning.

Ganesh tried to encourage her to return to her normal routine, but she remained withdrawn.

"I feel bad leaving you all alone. Why don't you let Jane come over?" Ganesh asked.

"I just—I can't—" The sadness overwhelmed her. "I wish my mother were here." Tears slipped silently down her cheek.

"Kavita," he said gently, wiping them with his thumb. "I don't need a baby to feel complete. I love you." He gathered her into his arms.

"I don't know who I am if I can't be a mother." She sobbed into his shoulder. "All the women in my family have been able to have children. Why can't I? What's wrong with me?" She sucked in several short gasps, trying to catch her breath.

Ganesh held her and reached a hand up to brush a strand of hair out of her face, tucking it neatly behind her ear. "It's going to be okay, you'll see. I know you miss your family. I miss mine too."

"I feel so alone. I—I wish we never came here."

"Shhhh—don't say that." He held her tighter. "It's going to be okay."

"You keep saying that, but I don't believe you." Tears continued to flow from her swollen eyes.

Ganesh walked her to the sofa and propped a pillow up behind her. He moved her embroidery basket within reach in case she wanted to do something to busy her hands.

"I need to get to work. Are you okay for now?"

She sighed and closed her eyes. "I don't know what I would do without you."

Ganesh placed a soft kiss on her cheek and turned to leave. "I'll be back tonight."

A few hours later, Jane came calling at Kavita's door.

"Sorry I couldn't come sooner. Ganesh told me—well." Jane straightened her shoulders. "How are you feeling today? Are you gaining your strength back?" Jane placed her bundle on the kitchen table, unpacking the lunch she had prepared.

"I'm . . . I'm okay. Ganesh has been so attentive . . . I—I just thought—I had hoped—" She broke down in fresh tears.

Jane rushed to Kavita's side at the couch, kneeled in front of her, and took her hands. "Kavi, don't despair. It will happen for you in the right time."

"I don't think that I have the strength to try again."

"Kavi, if I could fix this for you, I would do it in a heartbeat," Jane offered fiercely.

Kavita looked sharply at her friend, her eyes molten. "Do you really mean that, Jane?

"Of course. You're like a sister to me."

Silence stretched between them. Jane stood and busied herself with setting the table for lunch.

Kavita silently tracked Jane's movements around the kitchen. Her thoughts were racing with desire for the future. She was consumed with longing to feel the weight of a baby in her arms, to hear the soft patter of small feet on her floors, to look lovingly into the eyes of a little one staring back up at her. She rose and inched a few steps closer to Jane but did not close the gap completely. She knew what she was contemplating was enormous and life-changing but she had to say it. It was her only chance. Her eyes searched her friend's face for understanding. "Jane." She waited for Jane to look up from what she was doing. "Jane, Parvati has answered your prayers four times already and sent you four beautiful children. I could only hope for one such gift and you have been given four already."

Kavita paused, pressing her lips tightly together before she spoke again.

"If you should be blessed another time with a child, would you—could you find it in your heart to allow me to have that child as my own?"

Jane responded with silence, holding her breath. Kavita watched as the creases in her brow went slack.

"Oh—I, I'm sorry—I've asked too much." Kavita sobbed louder.

Jane moved closer and held her friend in a tight hug. It took several minutes until her crying subsided. "Kavi, I don't think I can have another child, but if I do"—she let out a long, slow breath—"I would be honored to let you raise it." Jane pulled back to look Kavita deeply in the eyes as she promised her best friend.

"Oh Jane." Kavita buried her head in Jane's shoulder and cried softly as she let her emotions wash over her.

CHAPTER 2

Jane

THE TEAKETTLE'S WHISTLE PIERCED THE silent morning air. Jane Simons moved leisurely about the kitchen. She would have to quicken her pace if she were to get the children fed and off to school. John had already left for the sugar mill hours ago. Her brood was scattered in various states of readiness. Her two boys were already dressed and collecting their schoolbooks while her two girls were nowhere in sight.

"Henry, Rudolph, where are your sisters? You will be late for school if they don't come to breakfast. Would you be a good boy and fetch them for me, beta?" Jane appealed to Henry.

"Last I saw, Betty was almost done getting dressed, and Emily was playing with her dolls," Henry answered. He hurried off to round them up. At ten years old, he was very protective of his two younger sisters, who were six and four. He watched over them for his mother, taking his role so seriously, so naturally, that he proudly took the lead walking them all to and from the schoolhouse each day. His older brother, Rudolph, just eleven years old, was far more aloof and preferred to walk at his own pace.

"Mama, did you make farine porridge today?" asked Emily, wandering in with a rag doll dangling from her hand.

"I started it. Come help me finish. I'm just about ready to add your favorite part," Jane encouraged.

Emily set down her doll and climbed onto the stool her mother placed next to the stove, so she was able to peer into the pot to help her mother cook. Jane allowed Emily to help her in the kitchen or anywhere else around the house that her daughter wanted. As the youngest, she was still treated as the baby and was afforded all the benefits commensurate with that special honor.

"Make sure you stir constantly like I showed you, so we don't get any lumps."

"I will, Mama," Emily purred. She added the sweet milk very slowly and continued stirring, waiting for the gentle bubbles to begin to form. The porridge began to thicken, and the scent of cinnamon wafted in the air. Her mouth started to water with anticipation.

Because they lived adjacent to the sugar plantation, they always had the freshest ingredients for Jane to make porridge. The cassava was plentiful and of the finest quality. Their family had been afforded the opportunity to purchase a small plot for their own farm when John's indenture contract was fulfilled. It had been a long eight years, but through a combination of backbreaking work and Jane's skillful budgeting, they had been able to save enough money to purchase the land. He continued to work for the sugar mill but was free to seek other employment if he desired. He supplemented his income with the produce they harvested from their family farm. However, finances had become more of a challenge since Emily was born.

Jane finished cleaning up the breakfast dishes and prepared to make her morning visit to Kavita's house as soon as the children were off to school. She'd had a strange, nauseated sensation when she was stirring the porridge and wondered if the milk had begun to turn. The children didn't seem to notice anything wrong with their breakfast, but she would have to make sure to check the milk again. She hated to waste food, but if it had gone bad, she would have to get rid of it. John counted on her to run the house efficiently, so she knew every penny counted. She was resourceful with what little they had, but there was no point in making everyone in the house sick.

Henry, Rudolph, and the girls hurried out the door to school. As she watched her children go, Jane could see the sun spilling over the verdant mountain side. The view from their house was lush with vegetation in all directions. You could see straight up the volcanic mountain when you stepped out the front of the house and from the other side you could see clear down to the ocean. A small smile of contentment spread across Jane's face.

"Bye, Mama." Henry waved back to her, glancing at his siblings to make sure they were not straying from the path. "I'll help you with your chores later this afternoon."

"You are so sweet, my beta, always worrying about your mama. Don't fret. I can handle my chores. You just concentrate on your schoolwork." Jane beamed with pride. She didn't want her children to struggle like she and John had when they left the severe poverty of India and came to this new land. Eager to forget the past, they had changed their names and given each of their children British ones to make it easier to assimilate. Kavita had been horrified; she'd felt that changing her name would be selling out her Indian heritage. Jane didn't agree. She was still the same person, but somehow the name change from Janvi to Jane allowed her to be more open to new ways.

Once the children were out of sight, Jane closed the door and hastily got herself dressed and dashed out the door to Kavita's house. On the way over, she thought about how fragile Kavita still was, but Jane believed in time she would return to herself. Jane hoped she hadn't made a mistake by promising what she had. When Kavita asked her for a baby, she was in a desperate state—and Jane felt a kindred desperation to give her *some* hope, no matter how remote the chances were, or perhaps *because* of how remote the chances. Jane suspected that she was close to menopause—her cycle had grown irregular over the last year or so—so there was virtually no chance of getting pregnant again.

When Jane arrived, Kavita was in her kitchen, just taking the kettle off the stove to prepare the chai, and turned to greet her. "Children off to school successfully?"

"They just headed out on their walk. Sorry for being so late this morning. I don't know what's wrong with me, but I can't seem to get out of my own way today," said Jane. She plodded into her friend's house, looking radiant despite her tardiness. Her long black hair swung as she entered. Usually she pulled it back into a loose braid that ran all the way down to her waist, but this morning she had left it free to flow gently around her shoulders.

"Oh, it's probably just one of those days. I wouldn't worry about it. You'll make up for it later if I know you," Kavita reassured her. "Come have some chai with me."

"Perhaps it will settle my stomach. I think I ate something that was about to go bad. I'm a little suspicious about the milk I used in the farine porridge this morning." Jane pulled out a chair and took a seat at Kavita's kitchen table. She slid the two porcelain teacups by their saucers closer to the edge of the table so Kavita could pour the chai for each of them.

"How are the kids doing in school? Henry still at the top of his class? He told me that he wants to be a doctor someday!" Kavita marveled as she set the teakettle back on the stove and took a seat to join Jane.

"He's doing so well. I guess it's a good thing to have lofty goals. I hope he can make it happen for himself. To be the first doctor in our family would be an amazing accomplishment! He is a dreamer but if anyone could do it, it would be my son," Jane said with a bit of trepidation in her voice.

Kavita raised an eyebrow. "Is everything okay?"

Jane moved closer and reached her free hand across the table to pat Kavita's. "Everything's okay. I'm just worried about . . . well, one just worries, you know." Jane's voice trailed off, thinking about how on earth they'd pay for medical school when money was already stretched so thin.

CHAPTER 3
Jane

MOST DAYS JANE BUSIED HERSELF with her sewing. Deft with a needle and thread, she was often complimented on the creations she made for her own children. Neighbors' requests that she make clothing for their children began to increase until she found herself with a small waiting list. Always an enjoyable hobby, she relished having found a way to make extra income to save for the future. With any luck, they might be able to give Henry a small amount of money until he could figure out a way to secure a college education. Jane had heard of some young men getting loans from universities if they pledged to work for the institution in some capacity, either while they were getting their degree or directly after they earned it.

Rudolph would most likely go into the family business of farming and not pursue a higher education. John was already apprenticing him. Thankfully, they didn't have to worry about the girls' higher education. A marriage contract for each of them would be arranged with a suitable man, carefully selected by Jane and John and agreed to by both families. This was the way it had been done for generations in India, and despite their embrace of other anglicizations, they were not about to break tradition in their new homeland. They lived in an East Indian enclave in St. Vincent where there were plenty of eligible young men from good families. Some had left St. Vincent to pursue greater opportunities on larger British West Indian islands, in Panama, or on the South American mainland. When the time came to find a bride, many returned to St. Vincent where girls like Elizabeth and Emily waited.

Despite the happiness of her own marriage, Jane remembered her own hesitation—fear, if she was honest—before the altar. She and John had decided that they wouldn't rush the girls into anything, giving them a little more time than they themselves had had.

John arrived home and greeted her quietly, more exhausted than she had ever seen him, an ashen look on his face. He set his bag down but still his shoulders drooped low.

"What's wrong, my love? You look as though your world has collapsed." Jane ushered him in the house.

"Sweetheart, one of the horses that we use to power the sugar mill had to be put down today. He had been showing signs of being overworked but I knew we had to make our production quota, so I kept pushing him—to his breaking point, it turns out." John slumped in his chair.

"That's not your fault, John. Animals have their limits."

"Yes, they do, and I should have known his limit before I pushed him beyond it. It *is* my fault."

"But you didn't—couldn't know," Jane stammered.

"It's my job to know. I failed him, and I failed the owner of the mill. Jane, you don't understand what this means." John paused and looked into Jane's eyes. "I will be held responsible for the cost of replacing the animal, and without the appropriate horsepower in the meantime, we will be falling well short of our production numbers. We can't afford this, Jane. We will be in debt for two years because of my miscalculation. We're barely making it now," he whispered. Jane saw his eyes close and squeezed his hand sympathetically, just as the children came barreling inside. Even as their raucous laughter split the tension, she knew that the conversation was far from over. They had to make some plans to get through this financial setback. "Just try to relax a bit. How about a glass of beer?" Jane started toward the kitchen.

"What's for dinner?" Henry pressed. Jane blinked. *Right, dinner.*

Although her appetite had left her, Jane prepared her stewed, curried chicken. It was John's favorite, and she hoped it would give him some comfort now. Jane called Emily to help her get the food to the table. The girl carried over the large plate laden with cassava bread for dipping into the rich flavorful sauce. When everyone was seated and Jane opened the cover of the tureen, she was suddenly overcome with a wave of nausea.

"Excuse me," she blurted out, rushing to the bathroom. Her stomach roiled as she retched violently, and she was struck with the realization that she had felt this way before—four times to be exact.

She barely made it until dinner was cleaned up and the children were off entertaining themselves.

"John, my love, can I talk to you?" Jane whispered gently.

"What is it?" John folded the newspaper over so he could see his wife just over the top of the fold.

"After what you told me today, I'm a little hesitant to tell you." She paused and tried to anticipate his reaction.

John's smile vanished from his face, and he set the newspaper to the side to give his full attention to his wife.

"I'm pregnant. At first, I didn't want to believe it, but I'm sure of it now." Jane walked closer and kneeled down in front of her husband. He took her hands in his, hung his head, and sighed heavily. They both sat silent for a long while.

"How did this happen?" John asked.

"You know how this happened—what kind of question is that?"

"You know what I mean—aren't we too old for this? I mean, how are you still—are, are you sure?"

"John!"

"Look, we're barely making it," he wheezed, "and it's my fault that things are going to get a whole lot worse."

"I'm sorry." Jane began to cry.

"Let's think about this a different way. Didn't—" He sighed, looking suddenly, deeply sad. "Didn't you tell me that Kavita was desperate to have a child?"

"Yes—but I, I don't know," Jane stammered.

John took her hands in his, but kept his gaze rooted to the table. "What if . . . what if we did agree to let Kavita and Ganesh adopt this child? We would be able to see her all the time and love her. We wouldn't really be giving her up. We could tell her the truth, that she is our flesh and blood."

Jane tried to pull her hands away, but he raised his gaze and held on to her. "Ganesh told me that he's fearful that she may never bounce back from her depression. Don't you see this may be a way that we can help the both of us?"

Jane looked into her husband's eyes as she considered what he was proposing. This was a serious life-altering decision, not only for them, but also for the child itself. What if the child didn't understand why they made the decision to give it up? What if they changed their minds but it was too late? Her mind was racing with all the possible outcomes and consequences. She *had* promised Kavita her next baby—a wild, shocking promise—what had she been thinking? But then, she never believed that she could become pregnant again, let alone that John might see her mad promise as their only hope.

Jane thought about the intensity of feelings that would inextricably lead to a love for the child growing in her belly. She knew from experience that a mother's love begins long before a child takes its first breath outside of the womb. If they had the baby right next door, they could not only keep an eye on it, but also help raise it if Kavita agreed. Jane already knew that Kavita would agree to anything if it meant she could have a baby.

John paced around the kitchen looking for the candles. Night was beginning to fall, and soon the entire plantation would be shrouded in darkness. "We have a lot to think about. It'll be at least a few weeks longer before you even begin to show." He fumbled for the matches and illuminated the room. "This child might have a better life than it could have with us. Just, just think about it."

CHAPTER 4

Jane

FOR SIX WEEKS, ALL SHE did was think, concealing her swelling belly from everyone they knew. It was not easy to hide it from Kavita, who saw her daily, but she managed to wear clothing that was loose-fitting and unbelted. If Kavita noticed her change of style, she did not mention it. It was agony, examining all the outcomes, and yet . . . she could see herself able to give her friend—her sister, really—the most precious, wonderful gift of a child while being able to live next door. It would not be like giving the child up completely, never to be seen again, endlessly wondering what had become of them. She would watch him or her grow up. She trusted Kavita to be a good mother; she'd been secondhand mothering Jane's own brood for years. She thought about them, her four children, and what she owed them. She had known extreme poverty in India and had come to St. Vincent seeking a better life, free from the hunger she had experienced. She promised herself that she wouldn't let her children go through that. She and John were flirting with disaster by bringing another child into the world. Her decision became clear to her.

"All right," she whispered to John one night in the quiet darkness of their bedroom. "We'll tell them in the morning." For a moment she thought he might already be asleep—until she felt his hand squeeze hers beneath the sheets.

The following morning while Jane was on her way over to Kavita's house, a cluster of spider lilies caught her eye. She bent down to savor their fragrant scent. They resembled the splayed legs of a spider but in brilliant white color. She gathered a few delicate stems and nervously walked over to Kavita's house.

"Mmmmm . . . it smells wonderful in here this morning. Are you cooking with cinnamon?" Jane asked, knocking on the open doorframe.

"I just finished a batch of tapioca and added lots of cinnamon. Come sit and have some chai." As Kavita turned around, she noticed the flowers in Jane's hands and remarked on how beautiful they were. "Is that pretty bouquet for me?"

"I spotted them on the way over and couldn't resist picking a few for your table. I knew you would enjoy them."

"You are positively glowing," Kavita complimented her friend.

Jane took a deep breath to explain, but found she didn't know where to begin.

"Neetu was here yesterday," Kavita prattled on, "and shared the good news that she is having her second baby. She and her husband are so thrilled. They are hoping for a boy this time since they have a girl already."

"Oh, that's so nice for them." Jane cleared her throat.

Kavita's smile disappeared. "I—I'm still a miserable failure at that part of life." She broke down into tears. "I'm sorry. You're probably sick of hearing me complain about this."

"My sweet friend, that's what friends—*sisters*—are for." Jane stepped inside, wringing her hands. "Kavita, I need to talk to you. I will—I *want* to deliver what I promised you, but I have some conditions."

"What—what do you mean? You can't be saying what I think you are, can you?" Kavita stammered, eyes wide.

"I'm pregnant again." Jane sighed heavily. "Ganesh probably already told you about what happened at the mill. John's in some trouble. We're working on a plan to repay what John owes but it won't be easy. We feel like we have the weight of the world on us."

"Oh, that's awful." Kavita wiped her tears.

"We thought because you and Ganesh desperately want a child, we could make this arrangement work for all of us." Jane reached over and took her friend's hands in her own and kissed them gently. "But we feel strongly that we want the child to know who we are. We don't want to lie and pretend that she didn't come from our blood. Can you agree to that?"

"Yes," Kavita said immediately. "Of course we can tell the child. I wouldn't dream of keeping the truth from them. We'll figure out a way." Fresh tears streamed down her face. "I'll never be able to repay you for this—this extraordinary gift. I promise I'll love this baby more than my own life!" She trembled as she rose from her chair and embraced her best friend.

Jane straightened herself up and held Kavita at arm's length away from her. Her smile wilted slightly. "This may not be easy for the child when they fully understand what we did. Are you and Ganesh prepared for that?" Jane asked.

Kavita gripped her hands fiercely. "I know it's complicated, but we all love each other. Surely the child will know this."

CHAPTER 5
Mahala

1910

Mahala took the time to complete the one hundred strokes with her hairbrush that her mother, Kavita, had taught her to do and dressed for school. She had hair the color of ebony and piercing brown eyes to go with it—as beautiful, even at age ten, as the magnificent Taj Mahal after which she was named. Tall for her age, she was surprisingly graceful, well-versed in manners and etiquette, which she was lucky enough to be taught by both of her mothers.

Grabbing her schoolbooks, she walked next door to find her siblings finishing their morning routine. "Mai bought me some candy," she said in a singsong voice. "It's too much for me to eat, so I'm bringing it to school today to share with my classmates. Do any of you want some first? You know brothers and sisters get first choice in my book." Emily and Elizabeth's eyes widened.

Just then Jane walked in the room, an eyebrow raised. "Mahala, that's very generous of you, but do you think your teacher will approve of you distributing all that candy to her class? It may cause some disruption to her lessons."

"Oh Mama, you worry too much. I'll sneak it to the other children so that it doesn't cause any problems," she reassured her.

Jane smiled. Mahala realized with a start that she now looked her mother eye to eye at full height.

When Mahala arrived at school, she began to hand out the candy Kavita had given her. The children were quietly delighted with the treat. She sat back in her seat, glad that she was able to bring something that was rare for her classmates.

The younger children started unwrapping the candy and popping it in their mouths. No one was paying attention to the lesson. Stiff paper wrappers crinkled. The aroma of chocolate drifted slowly to the front of the classroom, where Miss Singh noticed the unmistakable scent. She turned to discover that her entire class was completely enraptured—and spotted a wide smile on Mahala's face.

"Mahala, you can't go giving your classmates candy without permission," her teacher reprimanded.

Mahala wanted to make her friends happy, so she was embarrassed when the teacher admonished her.

"But Miss Singh—"

"You are disrupting my lesson," chided Miss Singh.

"I'm sorry, ma'am. Please don't be mad. I only wanted to share." Mahala's smile vanished.

"Sweetness, that was kind of you, but I have to ask you not to distract the students by your gifts," Miss Singh said with apology in her voice.

Mahala strode over to Miss Singh, hand outstretched with a beautifully wrapped chocolate.

"Please Miss Singh, don't be angry with me. I saved the coconut-filled chocolate for you because I know it's your favorite," Mahala cooed. A small smile spread across her face as her teacher softened.

At the end of the school day, Mahala and her best friend, Ruby, bounded out of the schoolhouse, almost tripping on the top step as they nearly collided with Mahala's sister, who was waiting for them for the walk home.

"Let's see how fast we can get home today. I want to go find some more shells for my collection," Ruby said, skipping faster, kicking dirt up in her wake.

"Don't bother going to your house, just borrow one of my bathing costumes so we can get there sooner! I'll race you!" squealed Mahala.

"Mai will be mad if you get your dress dirty, Mahala! Be careful!" warned Emily.

"Come on, quick, so she doesn't spoil our fun," whispered Mahala, her heart thumping.

The girls skipped home with their arms linked the whole way. Emily kept them in her sight despite their speeding ahead of her. They swept into the house as suddenly as a summer squall and dropped their pile of books with a great thud, changed, then dashed out again just as fast.

Ruby and Mahala galloped down to the beach. They made their way through the thicket of palm trees and shrubs, careful not to get snagged on the tiny thorns on the edges of the aloe vera plants that were abundant on the path. As they approached the beach, they saw a multitude of shells lodged in the wet sand. The water covered their potential quarry as it flowed back up onto the beach. "I saw a few small conch shells and lots of clamshells!" exclaimed Mahala.

A few minutes later, the girls' toes skirting the ocean waves, Ruby shrieked, "It's a tiger cowrie!" The tide was rolling in. Ruby bolted and scooped the spotted shell up before it was swept out to sea, grabbing a fistful of sand along with it. The hem of her skirt dragged across the beach, picking up wet sand and water like a sponge.

"Ruby, your skirt! Your mother is going to have your hide! Get out now!" Mahala yelled, running back above the tide. "Come on, there's no need to get our clothes wet when we have our bathing costumes underneath!"

"Look at my prize!" Clutching the shell in her fist, Ruby grinned right up to her eyes. She ran straight to Mahala to share her treasure.

"I've only seen pictures of them in Henry's seashell book. I don't think I've ever seen one in real life," Mahala marveled, wide-eyed.

"I'm going to polish this up and put this in my shell collection," Ruby said. She tucked it in her skirt pocket. The girls were so excited about Ruby's find that they decided to skip the swimming and continue looking for more shells on the beach before heading home.

When Mahala got home, she ran next door and bolted straight for Henry's room. On the bookshelf, she found the seashell book she was looking for. It was beautifully illustrated, with captivating facts on the lives of shells' inhabitants. She plunked the heavy tome down onto the floor of his bedroom and flung the cover open, perusing the colorful pages in search of the tiger cowrie. Dog ears marked where she had previously noted other appealing shells. An hour passed, then two.

"Mahala, are you still here?" asked Jane, popping her head in. "It's nearly dinnertime. Your mother is going to wonder what happened to you."

"Oh, I must have lost track of time. It's just that Henry has the most interesting books!"

"You're just like Henry was at your age," Jane chuckled. "He could never put down a book either." She picked up the newspaper from the sofa, folding it neatly and placing it on the side table.

"Miss Singh calls me a bookworm! She says that's why I always get the top marks in class!"

"I'm so proud of you, sweetling." Jane smiled broadly and wrapped Mahala in a tight hug. "Did you make sure to put it back just where you found it? Henry gets a little testy if his things are not just the way he left them."

She nodded. "I think so."

"Go home to your house, and you can come back tomorrow to continue your bookworm activities."

Mahala grinned. "Okay, Mama, I'll see you later." She skipped out of the house and swung the door closed behind her, daydreaming about being an oceanographer, like Sir John Murray. She remembered Henry telling her about Murray's breathtaking account from his *Challenger* expedition. Henry was fascinated by Murray's paper and had even managed to attend one of his lectures in Panama. She could see herself speaking at a conference where the room waited for *her* opinions with great anticipation. She would thrill them with her insight.

CHAPTER 6
Mahala

1913

LIVING ON AN ISLAND MEANT that Mahala was intimately connected with the beach. She loved everything about it and took full advantage of its treasures. This morning, she and Ruby ran down the well-worn path to the beach, their picnic basket bumping along behind them. As they approached the beach, they could hear the waves crashing against the sand and the subsequent rush of the water receding back to the ocean. "We should get a good ride today!" exclaimed Mahala.

The girls carefully removed and folded their dresses that they had worn over their bathing costumes and placed them beside the picnic basket for safekeeping. They quickly walked back to the inviting surf. The waves were fierce as they slammed against the wet packed shore. The girls jumped in, swimming fast, but were pushed and then dragged along the sand. Tiny broken shell fragments gouged into Mahala's delicate skin, raking up and down her legs, but she was not deterred by the scrapes. She convinced Ruby to venture out farther where the waves were bigger and provided the most fun. The undertow was strong, pulling them out even deeper, away from the shoreline.

Then Mahala's toes left the sandy bottom. Unable to touch, she and Ruby found themselves powerless to swim back against the current. Mahala's arms flailed as she bobbed up and down, gasping for breath before plunging underneath once again. Reaching to her for help, Ruby swallowed large gulps of water and coughed violently, only to suck in more water. Mahala thought they would surely drown.

Suddenly she felt a strong arm take hold of her waist. Someone instructed her to grab hold of her friend, and with a breath so welcome she cried, Mahala clawed Ruby to her side. Gripping her tightly, the stranger used his free arm to slash through the waves. Exhausted but victorious, they finally reached the beach. Both girls spilled onto the sand like two sea turtles washed up with the tide.

"Where did you come from?" choked out Mahala, gasping for breath.

"The last thing I can remember is that I prayed to Vishnu. Then *you* appeared!" gushed Ruby. "I will put an offering out to him as soon as we return home."

"Are you sure you two are all right? Are you alone down here or did an adult accompany you?" the man asked, catching his breath, one eyebrow raised.

"We're alone. We're old enough not to need chaperones," snapped Mahala. Turning to glare up at him, her eyes took in the man standing before her. He looked to be around Henry's age or a little older, maybe twenty-five or thirty. He was as tall and broad-shouldered as a god, despite being drenched in saltwater and littered with fragments of seaweed. His eyes were a deep cocoa brown, and his hair was a thick mass of ebony already drying in waves. His skin was the color of pale brown sugar, glistening as the sun refracted through the water droplets clinging to it. The sound of his voice broke Mahala's reverie.

"I didn't mean to insult you. I can plainly see that you are very independent young women. Why don't you gather your things, and I'll walk you home? Your parents will be grateful that they still have daughters to scold for returning home sopping wet!" he said, chuckling. "My name is Bharat Joshi and I'm very pleased to meet you both."

"We can walk ourse—"

"That would be nice of you," Ruby said quickly, cutting her off.

"Can we just start walking?" Mahala snapped.

"Fine by me. I love a brisk walk after an ocean rescue," he said, laughing again.

When they arrived at Mahala's house, they saw Kavita tidying up her garden in the front. Mahala skipped ahead to explain why they had a stranger with them. Kavita was relieved that the girls were both okay.

"Would you like to come in for a cold drink, Mr. Joshi?" Kavita offered.

"I appreciate it, but I really must get home. Would it be all right if I came back to call on your family another time?"

"Certainly. I'm just so grateful to you." Kavita shook his hand, giving him a wide smile.

"I have to run too," Mahala said talking a few steps away. "Bye Ruby. Bye Mr. Joshi. Nice to meet you . . ." She trailed off and went in search of her sister Emily.

It had been three weeks since Mahala and Ruby's near drowning. Since that time Bharat Joshi had made weekly visits to the Patandine house. Today, his gift to Mahala was a beautifully wrapped box of chocolates. Last week it was a fragrant bouquet of wildflowers, and the week before, it was two brightly colored silk ribbons for her hair. Mahala had come to look forward to Mr. Joshi's visits because she knew there would always be a special treat for her when he arrived. In addition, he was polite and complimentary and showed her the utmost respect when he came to call on the family. This afternoon he invited Mahala and her mother to accompany him on a carriage ride.

When Mahala stepped out of the house, she glimpsed the back of a horse harnessed to the carriage. He was a thousand pounds of pure muscle, with a gleaming jet-black coat and a long lustrous mane. Mahala had never seen such an exquisite beast.

"Mr. Joshi, what a beautiful creature this is. He looks like he should be pulling a carriage for a queen." Mahala beamed.

"Indeed, young miss, he will. His name is Midnight. Come, step up here." Bharat ushered both Mahala and her mother up onto the bench seat, seated himself, and secured the reins in both hands. He guided Midnight and his carriage through the streets around her Ratho Mill neighborhood. Mahala felt proud to be driven around in such a style. She liked the gazes she received from onlookers.

When the ride was over, Mahala was sufficiently pleased and wholly entertained. She thanked Bharat and bid him goodbye. She was still buzzing with happiness as she walked inside her house alongside her mother.

"Mai, don't you think Midnight was the most handsome horse you have ever seen?!" Mahala exclaimed, her eyes wide with excitement.

"Sweetheart, I didn't realize that you would be so taken with the man's horse," Kavita said with a laugh. "What did you think of the man?"

"I like him a lot, Mai," she said, glancing up at her mother, "I do. Will he come to visit us again soon?" Her eyes sparkled at the thought of another buggy ride.

"Yes, of course, my sweetling." Kavita smiled, then drew Mahala over to the settee to sit together. "Mahala, you—well, you are going to marry that man. Dai and I have already made the arrangements with his family and are drawing up the marriage contract. Your father is working on it as we speak. Dearest, we couldn't be more pleased that we were able to make this auspicious match!" Kavita declared proudly.

Mahala froze. She'd always known she'd be married off someday, no doubt to someone much like Bharat—but now? "Mai, no! I don't want to be married yet. I thought I would have more time." Her eyes widened. "Why are you doing this so fast?"

"Sweetheart, I . . ." Kavita brushed a long lock of hair from her daughter's face as Mahala recoiled. "Surely, you knew this day would come. Your father and I had our marriage arranged when I was just your age. I accepted *my* mother and father's decision and in time you will accept ours."

"But I—I'm not ready!" Mahala ran out of the room. Kavita's face drained of color.

∞

For two weeks after Mahala's outburst over the marriage arrangement, things were quiet. Peaceful, even. Mahala knew her parents were giving her time to settle down and get over her initial anger, and she, for her part, engaged in no further arguments. What they didn't know was that she had formulated a plan to deal with Bharat Joshi herself. She shared this with no one, not even her sister. She carefully calculated how to dispose of this problem, and she didn't want to be dissuaded by anyone, least of all good girl Emily.

Bharat Joshi came to call once again. As far as Mahala knew, they had said nothing to him about her resistance. Kavita escorted him to the garden. He held a large bouquet of flowers in his hand.

"Nice to see you again, Mr. Joshi," Mahala murmured, making sure to emphasize the formal title *Mr.* as she addressed him.

"Good afternoon, Miss Patandine." He extended the vibrant yellow and flaming red bouquet to her. "I brought you these Gloriosa Lilies because the striking blooms seemed appropriate for you. They remind me of your boundless energy and passion for life. Would you . . . would you do me the honor of a stroll about the grounds?" Baharat entreated.

Perfect, Mahala thought. *This is going to be easier than I planned.* Mahala obliged and followed him into the garden. Once they were out of Kavita's sight, he dropped to his knee and took her hand in his.

"Mahala, since that first moment I caught a glimpse of you on the beach, I knew I wanted to know more about you. I have enjoyed getting to know you better in these past few weeks and I hope you can say the same about me."

Mahala looked blankly back at Bharat. Part of her felt bad for what she was about to do to him. He was a nice man, just not someone she wanted to marry.

"Each week I prepare to come to visit you, I find myself dizzy with anticipation. Your beauty is unequaled by any woman I have ever known."

Mahala rolled her eyes. She kept her lips tight as she endured his lengthy, stupid proposal.

"You make me so happy to be in your company, and I can imagine a brilliant life for us with lots of children running around at our feet. I have come to realize that you are an insightful, respectful young woman with a passion for life that I haven't seen before in someone of your age. I hope you will be happy to know that I have secured your father's permission, as well as my family's, to ask you to be my bride." Bharat beamed, with pride in his voice.

Mahala had endured enough of this monologue. It was time for her to take action. She yanked back her hand from Bharat's clutch. "I will not marry you!" She spat directly into his eye and flung the flowers to the ground.

ꟹ

Bharat's face turned scarlet red, beads of sweat breaking out on his forehead. He quickly rose to his feet, brushed off his pants, and wiped his brow, then looked up and made eye contact with someone over Mahala's shoulder.

Her mother had caught the tail end of the disastrous scene from the gate and was now careening down the garden path toward them.

Bharat addressed her mother grimly, as if Mahala were invisible. "I don't understand how this could have gone so badly. You and Mr. Patandine gave your consent for this match, as did my own parents. I thought our courtship was going so smoothly." He squinted his eyes at them both. "I thought she would be happy about my proposal and excited to be engaged. Did I do something to offend her?" Kavita tried to answer, but he plowed on. "I know there are twelve years between our ages, but we could have a longer engagement. I'm willing to wait if I must."

Mahala bristled.

"I'm so sorry, Bharat, please forgive her," her mother interrupted, grasping Mahala's hand. "She's young and impulsive. I'm afraid that we've spoiled her a bit in allowing her to have her own way most of the time. I thought she was mature enough, but apparently I made a grievous miscalculation. I'll talk to her."

Kavita glared at Mahala. "Maybe we can fix this."

Mahala ripped her hand from her mother's and marched toward the house. As she stormed away, she heard Bharat's voice behind her.

"I'm sorry, too, Mrs. Patandine, but I . . . I must be on my way. Thank you as always for your hospitality."

Mahala slammed the gate behind her.

CHAPTER 7
Mahala

MAHALA BURST INTO EMILY'S ROOM and leaped onto the bed beside her sister, landing with such force that she knocked Emily to the floor with a startled shriek.

"What the . . . what's wrong, Mahala? Why do you have that awful scowl on your face?" Emily picked herself up off the floor and sat back down on her bed.

Mahala screamed face-first into the mattress, then turned a sweaty face toward Emily. "Mai and Dai have already arranged my marriage to that clod Bharat Joshi. I won't do it!"

"You told me you liked him!" Emily shot back. "He's been nothing but generous and attentive to you. Didn't you say you enjoyed the gifts he brought you over the past few weeks?" Emily cocked her head. "What did you think was happening with all his visits? You can't tell me you didn't suspect they were planning this."

"I *did* like him until I found out that they were planning to marry me to him!" fumed Mahala. "You can't tell me that it's not that bad because you haven't been put through this! You're seventeen, and Mama and Papa haven't sold you off yet!"

"Hang on, that's not fair. Mama and Papa are just taking their time to get my dowry in order. Plus, are you forgetting that Betty is already engaged?"

"It's times like this that make me wish that Mama and Papa didn't give me away."

Emily glared at her. "That's harsh. They did what they thought was right—and up until now, you're the one who got the better end of it. Who had a new dress anytime she wanted it? Who got to stay up late just because she needed an extra cuddle? Who got new toys when we all got hand-me-downs?"

"I know, I'm just—just—frustrated, I guess. Forget it. I took care of it myself," Mahala confessed.

Emily softened and curled up beside her, their noses practically touching. "What did you do, you silly girl?"

"Nothing. Well . . . I just made sure he would never want to marry me. He can't possibly face me after what I did to him in the garden today," Mahala said. "Anyway, I don't want to marry him, and that should count for something!" She sat up on the bed, crossing her arms tightly over her body and rolling her neck.

"Mahala," Emily sighed. "You've known for a long time that this was your destiny. This is the way it's been done for generations in our family. Look at how excited Betty is about marrying Alfie. She's happy with the choice that Mama and Papa made for her. It's different for Rudolph and Henry. But that doesn't mean it'll be bad, you know, being a wife, being a mother. I'm looking forward to it. I hope to have a half dozen little ones if my future husband agrees."

Emily embraced her sister gently, trying to soothe and reassure her as she pulled her close.

"Mama and Papa are working on a marriage arrangement for me now that Elizabeth's is set. It's just taking longer for me than for you. You're lucky, you know. You'll likely be engaged for at least a few years before actually having to get married. In that time, maybe you'll get used to the idea."

Mahala shook her head. "I don't want to insult you, Emily, but—" Her voice cracked. "But we want different things. I'm not ready to finish my education. I *love* school. I'm good at it, too. Just as good as Henry, maybe better."

Emily nestled her cheek against Mahala's hair. "You are the smartest person I know. That won't change just because you can't go to school any longer."

"Being intelligent doesn't mean anything if I can't do something with it."

"You will be bringing up children of your own someday. You can impart your wisdom to them."

Mahala's heart sank at the thought of imparting her wisdom to children before she could use and enjoy it herself. "I know, I know, and I do want to be a wife and mother someday," she said thickly. "I'm just . . . I imagined a way that maybe, just maybe, I could be the one to pick out my husband. There are people that do that, you know."

"Mahala, you can't pin your hopes on a fairy tale. You need to be practical." Emily gently squeezed her sister's shoulders. "You should be grateful for what you have. Your parents love you very much, both sets of them. Even if you weren't adopted by Kavita and Ganesh, Mama and Papa would have done the same thing. Maybe not at such an early age, but it definitely would have happened. You're so lucky, sometimes . . . sometimes I wish I could trade places with you." Emily drew back and looked Mahala deep in the eyes. "You have us all here as brothers and sisters, but you have your own space at your house, and you can virtually do whatever you want. They spoil you because they can. You should remember that."

Mahala sniffed and leaned her forehead against Emily's. She thought suddenly of how she was going to have to explain herself to her parents, of the sharp words she'd flung at Bharat in the garden. Her fiery temper had gotten the best of her again.

"Can I hide here a while longer?" she asked, laughing unevenly.

"As long as you like." Emily smiled. Two hours later Mahala quietly sneaked back to her own house, creeping around the kitchen for a snack to avoid her parents for a while longer.

The following morning when Mahala got up, she knew she had to answer for her behavior. She walked into the living room to face her father, whom she found at his desk bent over his correspondence. She quietly slid up to his side. She felt her stomach flip when she received his sober expression.

"Dai, I'm sorry for how rude I was to Mr. Joshi," she said, launching in resolutely before she lost her nerve. "I—I felt trapped. I didn't think I had a choice but to take matters into my own hands."

Ganesh replaced his papers onto his desk and paused. "Honestly, because you didn't continue to fight, we thought you had come to terms with the marriage arrangement," he admitted with a heavy sigh. "It makes no difference now. The situation is beyond repair. He withdrew his interest this morning."

Mahala bit her lip, the flood of relief she felt countered by her father's grim face.

"My dear one and only daughter," Ganesh went on, escorting her over to the sofa. "You know that marriages have been arranged in our family for generations. You are neither the first nor the last daughter that will be asked to accept this practice."

"I . . . I know," she said softly. "Can you forgive me Dai?"

His mouth twisted in a thin line. "In truth, your actions have serious consequences, and I don't know if our family's reputation can overcome this stain. You were thinking only of yourself," Ganesh said accusingly. "Your mother and I have always prided ourselves on our integrity and honor, trying to set a good example for you—and now what is our word worth? I will not excuse your actions, but I will have to explain them as having been caused by your youth and impetuousness. I requested a meeting with Bharat's father. I will have to offer a plausible reason for what you did if there is any hope of restoring the family's reputation."

Mahala sat still, accepting her scolding with her chin nearly touching her chest. She was ashamed of her behavior, but glad he wasn't going to make her reconsider. Mahala nuzzled up to her father and whispered, "I'm sorry, Dai. I love you."

Ganesh's furrowed brows released as his face relaxed. "I love you too, my sweet one," he whispered back as he wrapped her in a tight embrace.

Mahala dropped her crocheting into her lap, mesmerized by the sound of the songbirds and the constant whisper of the trade winds that drifted in the open windows as she waited for Kavita. She could hear the caw of the St. Vincent parrot rising above the soft trill of the yellow-billed cuckoo. She often played a game with her mother where they counted how many parrots they could spot on their walk into town—a game Mahala's shrewd eyes always won.

Finally, Kavita bustled in.

"I'm almost done with the tablecloth I'm making for you," Mahala announced.

"You'll have time, sweetling." Kavita moved to the sofa and patted the seat next to her. "Come sit near me. I want to talk to you about what happened."

Mahala blinked, stomach sinking as she settled next to Kavita. She'd known her mother was unlikely to let the situation go.

"I already got scolded by Dai, and told him I was very sorry," Mahala explained. "I—I wasn't trying to hurt this family. I would never do that. I love you and I love what we have here, just the three of us."

Her mother shook her head. "You are young, and you have much to learn that I can teach you, but you must start accepting the life that you were destined to lead. Your father and I have worked hard to ensure a good future for you, but it will only work if you behave as the young lady we expect you to be."

Mahala felt a sharp stab of frustration. "Haven't I done well in school? Aren't you proud of me?"

"Of course we are very proud of you."

"Why can't I do what Henry did? He didn't stop going to school after the sixth grade," she huffed.

"Henry's a man, and the expectations for men are different than for women," her mother said.

"That's not fair!" Mahala's face flushed hot.

"I know it doesn't seem fair to you now, but some day you'll understand."

"Both my brothers got a chance to see the world beyond this island. I want to do that too."

Kavita remained silent, pleading for understanding with her eyes.

"Even Emily and Betty had more time to be children before becoming wives," Mahala argued. "*They* were not asked to be brides at thirteen."

"Betty *is* getting married, and Jane and John are working on securing Emily's dowry right now."

Mahala rolled her eyes and blew out a heavy sigh. "I wish I was still their daughter," she spat out.

There was a long beat of silence before Kavita answered. "You'll always be their daughter, but you'll always be ours too. Your father and I love you very much. Nothing will change that. Tradition . . . tradition is important to us both. We don't want to forget where we came from or why we left." With that, she reached in her crochet basket and pulled out her hook and yarn.

Mahala knew that she had gone too far, but she didn't want to apologize. "I'm going over to see what Emily is up to." She packed her crochet project away and went next door.

CHAPTER 8
Henry

THE CARRIAGE PULLED AWAY AS Henry began the walk toward his family's farm, small valise in hand. The afternoon sun was starting to intensify, and small beads of perspiration began to form at his temples. He wiped them away with the back of his hand, lifting his hat slightly and repositioning it back securely on his head. He'd hoped he could make it home without soaking through his best traveling suit, and now decided it was wise to loosen his tie and remove his jacket, carefully folding it over his left arm.

He passed two men on the front porch of a neighboring house and nodded a greeting to them. One man rocked slowly back and forth while a cigarette dangled from the edge of his mouth; the other leaned against the doorframe, fanning himself with a folded newspaper and sipping what looked like a cool drink in a tall glass. The sight of that drink gave Henry an instant thirst, but he managed to put that thought aside.

It had been more than two months since he had seen his family, and now that he had almost completed his journey, a small smile spread across his face with anticipation of returning to his childhood home. Henry came to the crest of the hill and could just begin to see the two Soufrière trees standing with their arched branches and cascading red blossoms elegantly framing the modest house. He was suddenly struck by the memory of plucking some of those brightly colored flowers for his mother when he was a child.

After ambling up the stone walkway lined with spider lilies and small, deep green succulents, Henry tiptoed into the house, ducking slightly to fit his six-foot-one frame in the doorway. He carefully deposited his valise just inside, trying to make as little noise as possible, spying his mother scurrying around the kitchen, he snuck up behind her and whispered, "Surprise!"

"Oh beta, you nearly gave me a heart attack!" Jane clutched her chest and gasped as she dropped the wooden utensil she was holding. She opened her arms wide to embrace her son. "My sweet boy! I didn't expect you until tomorrow."

"I was able to trade in my ticket for passage on an earlier ship. It took a little more planning, but it was worth it." He squeezed his mother tightly and kissed her gently on the cheek.

"I'm so happy to see you! You're not in trouble at university, are you?" she asked, eyeing him suspiciously. "How did they let you leave early? I know how those old doctors are. They believe suffering is a rite of passage for you young medical students." Jane stretched her arms up as far as she could, but could not reach the large bowl on the high shelf. Henry instinctively stepped in to retrieve it for her without missing a beat.

"Mama, everything is fine. I left with official permission. I was able to get my work done early, and my professors were understanding. It's not every day your sister gets married."

She smiled. "We've missed you terribly. I'm just nervous about making sure you are following the rules. I don't want your scholarship to be in jeopardy. Your father and I are so proud of you. It's all—well, it makes it all worth it. Becoming a doctor, as you have always dreamed. Tell me everything!"

Just as the words left Jane's mouth, the door swung open, breaking the tender moment as Mahala bounded in, squealing with excitement. "Henry, you're home!" She launched herself into his arms. Henry swung her around a few times and deposited her gently down so he could get a good look at her. She brushed her dark hair out of her face and smiled up dizzily at her brother.

"How did you get so grown up? Are you sure Betty is the one getting married?" he teased.

"Stop! You're always playing!" Mahala chuckled. "You came home early so now you have to help with the preparations, too—there's no use trying to get out of it."

"Any suitors calling at your house yet?" Henry said with one eyebrow raised.

She gave him a frozen look. "That's a story for another day. Let's just focus on Betty for right now, okay?"

Henry darted around and tickled her to lighten the mood. "Come, help me put away my things."

Henry wanted to spend as much time as possible with his youngest sister while he was home. He knew that she had looked up to him growing up, constantly dogging his heels, asking him about his studies. Her curiosity often led her to leaf through his textbooks on science and literature. He was impressed at Mahala's ability to grasp things so quickly and knew that she would miss continuing her own education.

It was different with his brother Rudolph, who had left his schooling for prospects in Panama as soon as he was able. He was fortunate to have made contact with some agricultural businessmen upon his arrival and was able to start a successful farming operation there. Rudolph had sent his well wishes and apologies for missing the wedding, along with a gift which Henry delivered for him to the happy couple.

Henry walked into his room with Mahala trailing close behind and quickly noticed that the books on his bookshelf were out of order or outright missing.

"You can't resist stealing my books, can you?" Henry half joked, hiding his slight irritation.

"I can't get those books at school, and you don't want them anyway. Don't be mad at me," Mahala pleaded.

"I'm not mad, it's just I like to find my things the way I left them." He straightened his books to line up in size order, one inch from the edge of the shelf. "Hey, are you interested in an amazing discovery we learned about this term?"

Mahala tilted her head attentively. "What kind of amazing discovery?"

"A Dutch doctor invented a way to hear the electrical impulses of a person's heart from the outside of his body. His machine is able to detect those impulses right through the thickness of the flesh and bones! Until now, people have had to attach probes to the *actual* heart to capture this information. Isn't that astounding?" Henry looked wide-eyed at Mahala, waiting for her reaction.

"Did you actually get to see it working?" she asked eagerly.

"We saw only drawings of the machine and the patient hooked up to it in the medical journal. I hope to see it in action when I do my training at the hospital."

Henry dropped his valise, which was crammed with clothes and sundries, on the bed. He unbuckled its leather straps first and, after patting his pockets for the key, opened the dual locks, which sprang open as if with joyous release. Mahala began helping Henry remove the items from his overstuffed case. Just then the front door creaked open, and they heard the unmistakable footsteps of their father entering the house.

Henry turned and put a hand on Mahala's back and guided his sister out of his room. "Let me say hello to Papa. We can do the rest of the unpacking later."

CHAPTER 9
Jane

JANE HAD HAD TO MAKE several trips to the textile store in Kingstown before she'd found the perfect imported red silk and gold embroidery floss to make Elizabeth's wedding sari. Although they were of modest means, Jane wanted this to be special for her daughter. She adorned the dress with delicate gold beads along the hem and chose a thick gold band of lace to frame her head scarf. She also made the wedding clothes for the groom, a simple suit of ecru and gold.

Now, on the wedding day, Jane carefully gathered Elizabeth's wedding garments and accessories, including the traditional Indian brooch her own mother had given to her when she married John. She had decided to lend it to Elizabeth for her wedding as a special surprise.

She spread the sari across Elizabeth's bed, mindful not to put creases in the delicate silk. She then placed the jewelry on the center of Elizabeth's dressing table, adjusting things so that her brush and comb were fanned out to the right of the jewelry to make a dramatic presentation.

When her daughters entered the room to begin their bridal preparations, she caught Elizabeth's breath hitching at the sight before her. Her eldest daughter took a seat at the vanity and gently moved her fingers over the surface of the jewelry, feeling the polished edges and delicate indentations in the metal and the smoothness of the pearls. Jane was moved by the gesture.

Elizabeth reached for the comb and lifted it up to her sister behind her. Emily parted Elizabeth's glossy ebony locks down the middle, separating the two sections, braiding and pinning them into place. Mahala handed her the *maang tikka*, which Emily placed along Elizabeth's part so its oval pendant rested in the center of her forehead, suspended on a thin strand of leather strung with tiny pearls. Emily secured it with hairpins, brought both small braids together, and then gathered the rest of her sister's hair into a loose bun. When the girls finished, Elizabeth donned the lace-trimmed head scarf.

"Betty, you look incredibly beautiful . . . like a princess," John observed from the doorway of his daughter's room. His words hung in the air with the weight of the moment. Jane stepped back so he could come and cradle their girl's face with both hands. "I love you so much," he said, his voice catching in his throat. "You remind me of your mother on our wedding day, which seems like a lifetime ago. So much has happened since your mother and I started this journey together. We benefited from the wisdom of our parents choosing us for each other. It is my hope that you and Alfie will grow to love each other much the same way as your mother and I did." John gently gathered Elizabeth into his arms.

Tears slid down Elizabeth's cheek. "I trust you, Papa." She blotted her tears with a cotton handkerchief and returned it to her vanity table. John exchanged a knowing glance with Jane, gave her a wink, and pivoted on his heel out of the room. "I'll see if there is anything more to be done outside in the garden."

Jane sighed, reaching down for a necklace to drape on Elizabeth's neck. There was only a half hour left before her daughter would stand side by side with Alfie as his wife.

"Betty, do you promise me that you will always be my sister?" Mahala slowly bit her bottom lip as she slipped on the gold bangles that Kavita had given her to complement her emerald dress.

"Of course, silly. I'll always be here for you," reassured Elizabeth.

"First Rudolph left, then Henry left, and now you're leaving. I am happy for you to be starting your grown-up life, but I'm sad that we won't see each other every day any longer." Mahala avoided making eye contact and busied herself with tidying up the dressing table. Jane nearly interjected, but knew it was Elizabeth's fussing Mahala needed.

"I won't be far away. You can come and visit me anytime you want. Papa or Ganesh can take you over in the wagon. Come now, let's enjoy the day." Elizabeth took her sister in one hand and her mother in the other and walked into the kitchen with Emily trailing behind. The room was warm, every surface covered with food cooking in pots or cooling in serving bowls.

"Oh, yes, Henry's home—probably the real reason Mama has been cooking so much!" Elizabeth teased.

Jane raced around tasting her creations and adjusting the seasoning for each dish. The lid danced on her signature chicken curry, allowing the rich aroma to waft into the air, making her mouth water with anticipation.

Outside, Kavita was on hand to fine-tune the decorations. She directed Mahala and Ruby to hang paper lanterns in the garden on the side of the house and to place small vases with tiny bouquets on each of the tables that John had set up.

It was a small gathering, but it was exactly what Elizabeth had requested. She'd told Jane how important it was to her to be surrounded only by the people she loved most on her special day when she would become a wife and start a family of her own. Henry helped John and Emily greet the few guests they had, making sure they had enough room to accommodate everyone in their intimate garden setting.

Jane removed her apron and flung it over the back of her kitchen chair, dashing out of the room with just enough time to change into her dress. She did a quick walk through the house, peeking out at their reception tables. Everything looked perfect.

Just then, Emily brushed past Jane and called, "I just remembered that I need to lend Betty my favorite gold bracelet for luck." Jane couldn't help but notice a wince on Emily's face, the way her hands went to her midsection before she steadied herself using the back of a chair. Before Jane could ask if she was all right, she raced off to her room and returned with the jewelry. Emily smoothed her emerald dress while Jane tucked a loose tendril of hair behind her daughter's ear. Then they walked out to the garden together.

Outside, the air was filled with the unmistakable fragrance of flowers. Once the guests were seated, John announced that Elizabeth and Alfie were about to make their entrance. As they passed down the aisle, Jane was so pleased with the match they had made. She looked forward to grandchildren—many, if Elizabeth had her luck—in the future.

A week ago, Elizabeth had come to her and expressed her fears of not being able to conceive right away. Jane had reassured her that it would come naturally and not to worry, but it was obvious that her daughter was thinking about Kavita's difficulties.

Jane saw that Elizabeth was holding her breath and clutching her flowers tightly. She made eye contact with her daughter and smiled, hoping to relax her nerves. Just then, as if Jane had sent a telepathic message, Alfie leaned in close to Elizabeth and whispered, just loudly enough for Jane to overhear, "You're doing fine. Everything is going to be okay." Jane was glad that Alfie was trying to calm Elizabeth, but she could see the beads of perspiration at his temples and realized that he must be a bit nervous too.

CHAPTER 10

Mahala

As Elizabeth and Alfie exchanged their wedding vows, Kavita leaned in close to Mahala and whispered, "This could be you in a couple of years, my sweetling."

Mahala smiled obediently and replied, "What Elizabeth is doing—well, she's much better at that than I am."

"You could do it, too, if you set your mind to it." Kavita patted Mahala's hands resting on her lap. "You know that Dai and I want a good future for you, and that means making a good match."

"I want to be in control of my own life," Mahala hissed. "I want to meet a man of my own choosing in the right time. If you let me continue my schooling and go to university, I could—I could become a doctor like Henry. I could meet the right type of man that would be a good match for me."

"Sweetling, that decision has already been made. You must begin to learn how to run a household."

"Mai, please don't take school away from me," Mahala insisted a little too loudly.

Heads started to turn. Mahala received a sharp glare from the woman sitting next to her. She was in danger of spoiling Elizabeth's celebration, so she decided to retreat for now.

Elizabeth and Alfie started making their way through the small gathering of guests in the Simons family garden to accept their well wishes.

Jane stepped into the house, giving a quick flick of her head to both Mahala and Henry to signal that she needed their help to bring the food out for the guests.

The day after the wedding, Mahala was helping Emily tidy up her room when her sister suddenly dropped her brush. As it clattered to the floor, Emily reached for her abdomen and let out a guttural moan.

"Mama!" shrieked Mahala. "Come in here! Something's wrong with Emily."

Jane dashed into the room. Mahala could hear the water from the tap still running in the kitchen sink. "What's wrong, Em?" She dried her wet hands on her apron before she touched Emily lightly on the shoulders.

"It's not my time, but I'm bleeding again. I—I feel like a vise is squeezing my middle. It's been going on for weeks," Emily admitted.

"You hardly ate a thing yesterday," Mahala said as she held on to her sister.

"I'll send for the doctor immediately," said Jane.

An hour later, Doctor Kumar rushed in the door, his bag clutched tight in hand. Emily was curled up on her bed, holding Mahala's hand tightly. Jane hovered by the footboard. He started with a routine exam, taking her blood pressure, pulse, and temperature. Nothing seemed unusual. He then carefully palpated Emily's abdomen, beginning at the left side and moving across, and then repeated the process a few inches above and below the original horizontal path. "How long have you been experiencing these symptoms?" he asked.

"It's hard to say . . . At least a few weeks," Emily admitted. She squeezed Mahala's fingers as the doctor continued to assess the situation.

"There is definitely some tightness in her belly," he said, addressing Jane without taking his gaze off Emily. "But I think that is due to intestinal irritation. I'll leave her a small supply of aspirin for the pain, which should be taken as needed. You can also crush fennel seeds up and put them in her tea with a few drops of lemon juice for a few days, which should alleviate the abdominal discomfort. If she's not better by the end of the week, I'll return. Don't worry, she's young. She'll be right as rain soon." He collected his instruments and headed for the door.

Early the next morning, Mahala came in to check on Emily. "Are you feeling any better?" she asked.

"The pain is a little better, but I'm scared. Will you sit here with me for a while?" Emily asked.

"Of course. I'm not leaving you. Everything is going to be just fine. We're going to go down to the beach and toss seashells into the ocean in no time. You just have to rest and do what the doctor said. Do you want me to read to you? Do you remember where we left off?" Mahala grabbed the book off the bookshelf and began thumbing through to find the dog-eared page.

"I think it was chapter ten. Let's see what kind of evil Count Dracula is up to now." Emily chuckled.

A week later Emily was still suffering. Her belly tightened with intermittent cramps. She could barely keep anything down. Mahala never left her side. She had made a bed of blankets on the floor in Emily's room and only took brief breaks when her sister was sleeping to go back to her own house to change her clothes and grab something to eat.

Perplexed after his follow-up visit, Dr. Kumar arranged a consultation with the staff gynecologist at Kingstown General Hospital. Luckily for Emily, the hospital was fairly close to the Ratho Mill neighborhood. John transported her by horse and carriage as quickly as he could. Jane made the carriage seat comfortable for her daughter by stacking several blankets and pillows across the bench.

Mahala insisted on accompanying them and sat on Emily's right side while Jane was on her left. Jane wrapped one arm around her daughter's shoulder and lightly caressed her, her other fingers drawing ellipses up and down her forearm. Emily started to doze off, lulled by the repetition of the tender touch from her mother.

Mahala held Emily's other hand in her own for the entire ride. "You remember when we built that flower fairy house in your garden?" she said gently. "It had the most beautiful colors. We found so many little sticks to make the walls of the house, and then we used tree bark for the roof. We had to break some of the sticks so they would all be the same size. You insisted that we couldn't have a house with lopsided walls." She chattered on to fill the silence in an attempt to keep Emily's mind—and her own—from worrying about her condition.

Emily simply had to recover, Mahala thought. The alternative was too frightening to imagine.

The hospital's gynecologist ordered a second consultation after his examination—this time, an oncologist. Both doctors approached Jane, John, and Mahala in the waiting room.

"Mr. and Mrs. Simons, can we speak in private?" They looked meaningfully at Mahala.

"Mama, please, I want to know what's going on with Emily. You don't have to shield me from the truth," she pleaded with Jane.

"Okay, you can stay." Jane reached her arm around Mahala and pulled her close.

The doctors appeared to exchange an uneasy glance. "I'm Dr. Williams and this is my colleague, Dr. Taylor," the taller one began. "We are so very sorry to have to tell you this, but your daughter is in the advanced stages of ovarian cancer. What we believe to be the original mass has grown to the size of a peach on her right ovary, and there is evidence that it has begun to spread to her lymph nodes as well. I'm afraid that surgery is not an option for her." Mahala felt her vision flicker for a moment as panic gripped her.

Jane recoiled, stepping on Mahala's foot. "I—I don't understand. Dr. Kumar said that it was an intestinal problem. It's only been a matter of weeks that she's been in pain. Why can't you remove it through surgery?"

"As I said, Mrs. Simons, it has already begun to spread away from the original mass into the surrounding tissue and lymph nodes. Even if we did operate, it would not get all the cancer, and she would have a long and painful recovery from the surgery itself without the benefit of a cure."

John's grip on his wife's hand tightened as she began to tremble and sob. "What can we do for her?" he asked. Mahala felt numb.

Dr. Williams took in a deep slow breath and collected himself. "If she were my daughter, I would take her home and make her as comfortable as possible. I'm so sorry. There's really nothing more, medically speaking, that we can do for her here. We'll give you some time to process this news, and then we'll discharge her when you are ready." Both doctors turned and strode through the hinged hospital doors, leaving them swinging in their wake.

Jane sank slowly into John's shoulder and pulled Mahala with her as she leaned. John reached around them both. "How could Kumar be so wrong?" Jane sobbed. "He assured me that she would recover."

Mahala's thoughts were racing in her head. These doctors had to be wrong. She was unable to fathom life without Emily.

"We should have brought her to the hospital immediately. Kumar is incompetent! He should have recognized the symptoms for what they were!" John barked.

Just then, a nurse approached with sympathetic eyes and what was likely discharge papers in her hands.

Mahala looked up at the nurse and then at Jane. "Will you be okay if I go sit with Emily while you and Papa sort this out?"

Jane squeezed her eyes shut and nodded. "She needs you now more than ever."

Despite everyone's prayers, Emily continued to decline. She began losing weight along with the strength to move around freely. Eventually, she was unable to get out of bed. Her meals were brought to her. Mahala was the only one who could get her to eat at all.

"Here, Em, open your mouth now and taste Mama's chicken soup," Mahala encouraged her sister. She slowly lifted the spoon to Emily's mouth and placed a napkin underneath in case she rejected it. Her sister opened her mouth with great effort and accepted the proffered spoon. Mahala saw how hard it was for Emily just to swallow a small amount of the tepid liquid.

Dipping the spoon back into the broth, Mahala sang the Hindi song that both their mothers sang to them when they were infants. "Mama chata daia . . . dupaia. Dudu pata lilyow . . . hamar beta kamumai katali katukshani." She elongated the last word—"ka-tooooooksha-ni." The familiar rhyme meant, "Mama has something special for you. Here it comes. Open up and doooown the hatch."

Emily's eyes welled up. She reached out and squeezed Mahala's hand.

"It's going to be okay, Mahala, you'll see." Tears slid down her cheek and started to collect in the fold of her slender neck. Mahala dabbed her throat and brushed her cheek with the napkin to wipe them away. Then she reached up with the back of her hand to dry her own eyes.

"I love you. I want you to know . . ." Emily trailed off.

Mahala cut her off. "Don't say that. I know you love me, and I love you too. You're not dying." Even as she said the words she knew they were a useless lie. She knew her sister did not have much more time. Emily was just eighteen. She had barely had time to live her life, and now it was being taken away from her before she could realize her dream of marrying and creating her own family. It simply wasn't fair. Emily did everything right. She was the obedient child, a loving sister who took her family responsibilities seriously. Mahala thought bitterly about how Emily *wanted* the destiny—the husband, the children, the household—that Mahala couldn't bring herself to face. She would never get it, while Mahala couldn't escape it.

Emily took a deep slow breath. "Can you bring me my jewelry box?"

Mahala went to the vanity table. The small wooden box was carved with an intricate scrolling design interspersed with tiny leaves and stained a rich mahogany color. She picked it up and cradled it heavy in both hands, respecting the items contained within. "Would you like me to open it for you?" Mahala asked.

"Bring it closer to me."

Mahala lowered it down to Emily's outstretched hands and let it rest on her lap. "It's not too heavy for you, is it?"

"No, I can manage. Come sit here with me." She patted the bed, inviting Mahala close to her so they could look into the box together. She lifted the lid up and back, resting it on its hinges. Her fingers clumsily searched its contents until she pulled out the gold bracelet Mahala remembered her lending Elizabeth for her wedding. She handed it to Mahala. "This is the bracelet that Mama and Papa gave to me when I was just about your age. It was my twelfth birthday. Mama was consumed with her sewing, trying to finish a dress for one of our neighbor's daughters, and Papa was working late at the sugar mill. I really thought they had forgotten about my birthday. But when Papa came home, he was carrying a small cream-colored silk bag closed tight by a drawstring. That night they gave me this. It's beautiful, but what I love best about it was what it means." She took a rasping breath. "Mama explained to me that they had selected this gift because its shape symbolized the way they loved me—infinitely—without end. I—I want you to have this bracelet, this perfect circle. When you wear it, you will always know that my love for you will never end." Emily held the bangle out to her sister.

Mahala openly wept this time.

Three weeks later, Emily was gone.

Mahala was inconsolable. She desperately missed her sister and blamed the doctor for not curing her. She spent every spare minute she had over at Jane and John's house. They tried to support each other through the immense grief they all felt.

Mahala tried to fill the void that Emily left in everyone's lives, but, outspoken by nature, she was very different from her shy, unassuming, reserved sister. Overwhelmed, Mahala felt weighed down by the grief, almost like it was pulling her down into a great crevasse. The life Mahala had counted on sharing with Emily had evaporated with her sister's last breath.

CHAPTER II

Mahala

1918

Mahala and Ruby were at Ruby's house in her sitting room with baskets of yarn staked between them. Ruby worked each stitch between her thumb and forefinger with the crochet hook positioned in her right hand. With her left, she looped the cotton thread around her other forefinger and held the tension between her left thumb and middle finger. Her lips tightly pressed together in concentration as she willed her fingers to move in a familiar rhythm. She carefully yarned over each chain with her right hand until she counted the nineteen stitches she needed to complete the center circle of each flower in her pattern. She had finished ninety of the ninety-six flowers she needed. It took patience and dexterity to join all the flowers together in order to produce a proper tablecloth.

Mahala sat observing, in awe of the speed at which Ruby crocheted. She had her own project of a far smaller scale.

"It's as if your fingers have a mind of their own. How *do* you work so fast without making mistakes?" Mahala asked.

"I've been doing this so long it just comes automatically to me. I don't even really think about it except for the counting. Sometimes I'm even surprised when I've completed so many pieces that my basket is overflowing. Then I know it's time to start joining them together," Ruby answered.

"At this rate, you should be finished in time for your departure to New York."

"That's the idea. I still have five days to go, but I am focused like a machine. I can't wait to see Jerome. It's only been a month, but I miss him like crazy," Ruby said.

"Couldn't he have waited for you so you could have gone together?" Mahala asked.

"No, not really. His uncle got him a job as a butcher's assistant, and he had to start right away—otherwise the job would be offered to someone else. And he wanted time to secure a seamstress job for me, too, because we'll need two salaries to afford the apartment that his uncle found for us. It's in East Harlem, part of Manhattan. Can you imagine an island girl like me living in a place as grand as Manhattan?" Ruby's eyebrows shot up.

"Hey, Manhattan is an island, too. You'll fit right in," Mahala said, laughing. "You must be bursting to see your husband again. I'm so happy for you that you'll finally be together." Mahala continued to move her crochet needle over and through her yarn. She had nearly completed the doily she was working on.

"I am excited—but nervous about the journey."

"We've been on the water our whole lives. Just think of it as an extra-long boat ride with a huge bonus at the end."

"Mahala, it's five long days on the open ocean. We leave from Barbados on Monday, and we don't get to the port of New York City until Saturday." Ruby inhaled a deep breath and blew it out slowly. Her fingers never stopped flying through her stitches. "My cousin is going to accompany me, so that makes me feel a little less scared about the voyage."

"You will do fine. I'd be beyond excited to trade places with you and go to New York. I envy what you and Jerome have. He is so sweet and really cares about you."

"You're still as headstrong as ever. I feel sorry for the man who will be your husband one day," Ruby teased. "Honestly, though, Mahala . . . I don't know any eighteen-year-old girl who is not either already married or promised to be married." Mahala opened her mouth to protest. "I'm not trying to insult you, but you are too independent-minded for most men. They are not looking for a partnership. They want someone to take care of them and their family. You want to *run* the family as well as your own life!"

"I don't want to be pushed into a marriage with a man who is going to try to be my father. I already have two of those. Three if you count Henry. My whole life, everyone has been trying to tell me what to do."

"Let's be honest, Mahala, you haven't always listened."

"You're right, and I'm determined not to give in on this either." Mahala's eyes narrowed as she raised one eyebrow. She gathered her unfinished doily and tangled yarn and placed them inside the basket. "Come on, let's take a break and go down to the seaside. It won't be long before you are caught up with bustling crowds and motor cars. I've seen pictures of the streets of New York, and it doesn't look anything like our island." She stretched a hand out to Ruby and gently pulled her up from the sofa.

They found their two bicycles leaning against the side of Ruby's house and walked them away until they got clear of the low-growing grasses. Mounting their well-worn leather seats, they tucked the bottom half of their knee-length cotton dresses between their thighs, but the lightweight paisley-print cotton still fluttered in the wind as they gained speed down the hillside to the coast.

Mahala hurriedly dressed, pulling on her skirt and slipping into her eyelet lace blouse. She'd woken up later than she planned, but she still had time before Ruby and her parents would be leaving for Kingstown.

Earlier in the week, she'd accompanied Ruby on several errands in preparation for her trip. They'd gone to the bank to change her stash of British pounds to US dollars and then to the post office to send a letter to Jerome.

Now the day was finally here, and she had to focus on saying a proper goodbye to her best friend. She gently raked her hands through the bucket that contained the shell collection she and Ruby had accumulated over the years. She always kept her half on the bottom shelf of her bookcase. Now Ruby had left hers with Mahala for safekeeping, since she could not bring the shells to New York.

Mahala searched for that extremely rare tiger cowrie that Ruby had found years ago—just before Bharat saved them. She knew it was in there but didn't want to dump them all out of the bucket for fear of damaging the fragile ones. She had sifted about a third of the way down when she caught a glimpse of the unmistakable spotted burnt brown and white shell. She plucked it out of the surrounding treasures. Each shell had meaning to them both, but this one in particular meant so much to Ruby. Mahala thought it was the perfect parting gift. She wrapped it in a sheet of newspaper and tucked it deep into the side pocket of her skirt.

She heard Ruby's signature knock at the door, one rap, pause, then three successive, staccato raps. Mahala smiled wide when she opened the door to find her best friend.

"You came here? I thought I was meeting you at the dock!" Mahala embraced her tightly. They walked out arm in arm to the carriage loaded with Ruby's two large trunks. She tried not to contemplate the creeping feeling of finality, pushing it from her mind.

On the way to Kingstown, the two friends sat side by side across from Ruby's parents. Mahala reached into her skirt pocket to retrieve her gift. She handed the small, folded paper package to Ruby and waited silently for her to recognize the prize she had taken such delight in finding many years ago.

"The tiger cowrie! Mahala, I meant for you to have it and keep it safe for me." She cradled the glossy shell in the palm of her hand, feeling its smooth dorsal surface and toothed groove in the center of its underside. "According to African legend, cowrie shells represent the goddess of protection and are connected with the power and strength of the ocean," Ruby said.

"That's exactly why you need it more than I do. Take it to New York, and you will have the power of the ocean with you always. You will remember me and the island always."

"Your friendship means the world to me. I will treasure this forever." Ruby squeezed Mahala in a tight embrace and then wiped the tears from her eyes with the back of her sleeve.

CHAPTER 12

Mahala

SATURDAY MORNING HAD BECOME A special father-daughter time for Mahala and Ganesh to sneak out of the house early, while Kavita was still asleep, and go to the market to bring home some fresh fruits and vegetables. They both enjoyed that it was just the two of them. Because Ganesh worked so many long hours, Mahala appreciated that he chose to spend this time with just her.

This Saturday was no exception. Mahala rose early and found her father in the kitchen sipping his tea and waiting for her. The ride into town was pleasant, and once they parked the wagon, they stopped at several produce stalls to look over the fruit. Soon the crate Ganesh had brought was almost filled to the top.

Mahala called out to her father. "Dai, do you mind if I just slip around to the fabric store to get some things? It will only take a few minutes."

"No, of course not. You go get what you need, and I'll load this into the wagon while I wait for you."

Ganesh walked toward the busy street, his arms laden with the wooden crate filled with cassava and breadfruit. Not watching where his feet were going, he was jolted down six inches off the curb and lost his balance. He lurched forward with the crate barely still in his hands, fighting to regain his balance, as a greenish-yellow breadfruit rolled out into the middle of the street.

Suddenly, a merchant came careening around the corner. His horse deftly maneuvered himself to avoid running over the man, but the cart hitched behind it could take no such course. At full speed, it collided with Ganesh, smashing into his body and throwing him under the wheels. The merchant was catapulted from his seat and crashed to the ground. He looked up, blinking several times in rapid succession to focus on his surroundings. His hands instinctively went to his head to calm the pulsing pain pounding from the inside of his skull. His first thought was of his runaway horse and broken cart. He then remembered the man he had run over and scanned the street for sight of him. He saw someone in a crumpled heap, face down.

People began to gather around Ganesh. Blood trickled from his head, spreading over the road and seeping into the hard-packed dirt surface of the thoroughfare. One of the men reached down, gently turning Ganesh on his side to see if he was still breathing. He felt a faint breath coming from his mouth.

"Can you hear me? Are you all right? Can you tell me your name?" the man urged. Ganesh could form no words.

Just then, Mahala rounded the corner. She had heard the commotion from inside the fabric store but didn't step out to investigate. Unfortunately, accidents were a common occurrence on the busy market street. Having finished her quick errand, she'd come back to meet her father—only to find several onlookers crowded around a badly banged up form of a man. As she got closer, she recognized him.

"Oh, *no*! No, no, no! This can't be happening," she shrieked. "Dai! Dai!"

"We need a doctor as soon as possible," shouted a man, suspecting that the injury was too great to survive. Mahala clung to Ganesh's side as strangers brought the closest wagon around.

Kavita burst through the Kingstown hospital doors and looked frantically for any hospital staff member she could find. She rushed to the admitting desk. "I'm looking for my husband, Ganesh Patandine. He was brought in with a severe head injury."

Mahala jumped up from her seat in the lobby and ran to her mother's side. "Mai, it's me. I'm here. I'm waiting for the doctors to tell me something."

Kavita turned to look at her daughter. "Sunil next door told me that Dai got hit by a cart when you were in town this morning. How is he? How badly was he hurt? Do you know anything?" Kavita blurted out in rapid succession.

"Mai, I don't know anything yet." Mahala gently led her mother over to the chairs directly in front of the reception desk. She eased her into the seat and took the other next to her all in one fluid motion, never taking her hands off her mother's arm.

Kavita resisted, trying to rise out of her chair. "I have to find out how he is! I can't just sit here!"

The receptionist cut in. "I'll let Dr. Burton know you are here. He will update you on your husband's condition."

"Mai, you have to remain calm." Mahala tightened her grip on her mother's arm, tethering her to her side. "She said the doctor would be out to let us know what his condition is."

The emergency room doors swung open as Dr. Burton pushed through and strode over in the direction of the Patandine women. Immediately they both rose to meet him. Kavita could tell that it was not good news by the way Dr. Burton approached them. His eyes were full of sympathy, and his mouth was set in a straight line. He reached out his hand, placed it lightly on Kavita's shoulder, and took a slow inhale before speaking.

"Mrs. Patandine, I am so sorry. Your husband's injuries were too great. There was nothing we could do to save him."

Mahala felt her mother's knees buckling and took hold of her with both hands. Sinking to the floor, they wept for the father and husband that they had lost.

Months after the horrifying accident, Mahala muddled through her days, continuing to tutor her young students and often longing for some distraction from her grief. When she woke early this morning, she made breakfast for her mother. She left it covered on the stove with a note she placed on the kitchen table, telling Kavita that she was going over to Jane and John's house.

Mahala found Jane in the kitchen making her own breakfast.

"You're up bright and early this morning," Jane sang out. "Have you already eaten? I could fix you some breakfast if you want."

She hadn't had much of an appetite for months. "I'll just have some tea." Mahala reached into the cabinet, grabbed an extra cup and saucer for herself, and slid into a seat at the kitchen table.

Jane glided from the stove to the table with the teakettle in one hand. She poured the steaming tea water into Mahala's cup and handed her the sugar bowl. "You'll never forget him, you know. Or how much you loved him."

Unexpected tears streamed from Mahala's eyes. "I lie awake for hours, unable to make my brain stop spinning. When I finally do manage to fall asleep for a short while, it all starts again as soon as I open my eyes." She left her teacup untouched. "It's brought my grief from Emily back too."

"Many years ago, when I lost my grandmother, my own mother explained to me that the hurt I was feeling was so intense because I had loved her so much. The depth of grief is an indication of how much we truly loved someone." Jane sat down at the table and took Mahala's hands in her own. "It's why I nearly drowned the day we lost Emily."

"Your mother sounds like she was a very wise woman." Mahala gave her a weak smile back.

"I see a lot of her in you. You have her vibrance and passion for life. We will all help to keep Ganesh's memory alive. I promise."

John chimed in from the doorway. "I miss him every day too. Why don't we try to think of a way we can all honor him together? Would you like that?" he asked.

"Yes, I would. Thank you, Papa. That means a lot to me." She wiped a tear from the corner of her eye.

CHAPTER 13

Jane

"It's been too long since you came home. Come, beta, tell your mama how her grandchildren are doing. Your daughters must be a sheer delight," Jane said, smiling sweetly at Henry. "I know we've missed quite a bit since the last time you came home."

"I'm pretty sure that Sofia already knows more than her second grade teacher, and Lily is the pride of the whole schoolhouse, even though she's the youngest child there. She's always being held up as the example of how to behave and she beams with pleasure when she recounts the stories to us at home. How about next school vacation I bring the girls back with me to visit you and Papa?"

"That would be so nice and then we could also see that lovely wife of yours," Jane said. "How is Violet? Is she well?"

"Well enough. The girls keep her busy and she has a lot of responsibility running the house, not to mention being a doctor's wife. She's on call as much as I am in the community. People think they can get to me faster if they stay on her good side." He sighed deeply. "Sometimes I feel like I'm asking too much of her, and I fear that she's not happy with the choice she's made in becoming my wife."

"Nonsense, beta." His mother batted his shoulder.

"I don't know, Mama, she gets so irritated with me when I have to work late or if I have to visit patients who can't make it into the city. A few months ago, I treated a woman that required me to be away from home for several days on multiple occasions. She had severe kidney stones and was in agony for days at a time. Each recurrence, the woman's family pleaded with me to stay to see her through the difficult part, which I obliged. But Violet glared at me when I returned home and wouldn't speak to me for almost a week."

"Your marriage is your own business. You are a grown man, after all . . . Did she have cause to be jealous?" Jane raised her eyebrow and tilted her head up at her son, who stood a full foot taller than her.

"Mama, no. I love her, and I always return to her," he insisted.

"*Return* implies that you have strayed from her. You don't have to tell me. Again, it's really your own business, but be careful and think of those two beautiful girls. You wouldn't want anything to jeopardize your family," Jane advised. "Let's have a nice cup of tea so we can have a proper visit." She ushered him into the kitchen, where John was already seated at the table.

"Any eligible bachelor friends that you can introduce your sister to?" John chimed in. Mahala was now nineteen; while the occasional prospects had come and gone, none had stuck. Everyone in the family knew there was some urgency to getting her marriage arranged.

"Actually, Papa," Henry replied, brightening, "I may have someone in mind. I will do my best, but you know how willful she can be." Jane turned, listening intently.

"Promise me something, Henry," his father said.

He looked up, eyes darting to Jane first, then John. "Anything, Papa. What is it?"

"If something should ever happen to me, I want you to look after Mahala. When she lost Ganesh, she still had me to step into the role of her father. She is my flesh and blood, after all, and I will always try to do what is best for her. Kavita has been struggling since Ganesh died."

"Of course, Papa. But why are you saying this? You aren't sick, are you?"

"No, Henry, I just want to make certain that you know what your responsibility is. Rudolph is, well—*you* are far more willing and capable of taking control of the family if necessary. That's all." John cleared his throat.

Jane stood up abruptly, attempting to break up the awkward conversation. "Hey, how about you two bring in some of the bagasse so we can have a nice fire?"

Henry and John got up in unison and walked out to the shed. Jane smiled to herself, as she noticed the father and son duo slipping into the old familiar rhythm they had with each other since Henry was a boy.

CHAPTER 14

Jane

1919

JANE STOOD IN HER KITCHEN, hands trembling, reading Henry's letter for the second time. She reached for the table to steady herself, sinking into the chair to absorb the words on the page.

Henry Simons
Colon, Panama
Dear Mama and Papa,

I know you may be shocked to learn that my marriage to Violet is over. The details are too great to explain in this letter. Suffice it to say, the situation requires immediate action. I need you to come to Colon and fetch Sofia and Lily at once. Violet is intensely angry with me and threatening to take the girls away from me forever. As you can imagine, I cannot allow this to happen. I must act swiftly but having just taken leave last month, I cannot leave the hospital or my patients presently. Please come at once. I have enclosed a sum of money which should be enough for your passage on

both the ferry to Barbados and the ship to Colon. Do not delay. The fate of my daughters rests in your hands.
Your loving son,
Henry

Jane dropped the letter on the table and dashed out of the house, leaving a ripple in the air that caused the thin paper to hover above the table before it floated side to side to the floor. She found John out in the garden. "Henry's in dire need of our help! I have to get to Panama immediately!" Jane blurted out.

"Slow down. What's the matter?" John looked up, holding his hoe in one hand and wiping his brow with the other. "Tell me what's happened."

"I just received a desperate letter from Henry asking for our help. He says that he fears Violet may take the girls away from him. He needs us to bring them here until he can figure out what to do." Jane's arms cut wildly through the air.

"Why would Violet take the girls from him? What did he do?" John asked, startled. "Do you think he did something to her? I mean, could he . . . would he . . ." He trailed off.

"No! He wouldn't lay a hand on her, John. You must know that." Jane's eyes narrowed, piercing her husband like a hot poker. "How could you even think that of our son?"

"I don't know, Jane, I'm just trying to figure out what could have gone so terribly wrong in such a short time. When he was here last month, he didn't say anything about any trouble with Violet, did he?"

"Well, not specifically, no," she admitted. "He did mention that she was irritated with him for seemingly paying more attention to his patients than his family." Jane began pacing back and forth, her long braid swaying each time she changed direction.

"Look, our son is a good man, I'm not saying he's not, but he does have a need to always be in control. Violet and the girls have, for the most part, benefited from his ambition and decisiveness—but ambition can blind one to one's weaknesses. The girls are still young, and they need both a mother and father living in the same house," John argued.

Jane's heart squeezed. "John, you're not listening to me. The marriage is over, he says. We have to help those girls."

He looked at her grimly. "Is it beyond all hope?"

"So it seems," she said, her eyes wide. "I'll let you read the letter so you will understand Henry's desperation. He wants us to leave for Panama as soon as possible. Surely it was difficult for him to admit this, to ask us for this. It is imperative that we help him!"

John nodded. "You will have to make the trip alone, my love. I can't possibly leave now while I have so much to do with the farm. Do you feel up to it?"

"I absolutely can, if you can book the passage for me. It's such short notice."

"Of course, my love, I will do what I can. Let me just finish up here first."

She walked reluctantly back to the house as John finished preparing the soil, making the last of his neat rows with his hoe. She could tell his concentration was broken; Henry and his granddaughters were now certainly foremost on his mind. He would have to plant the seeds tomorrow.

∞

The following day John made arrangements for Jane's trip to Panama in two days' time. There was no direct way to get to Panama from St. Vincent. She would have to take the ferry from Kingstown over to Barbados and then a larger ship to the port of Panama City—a journey that would take another three days before her granddaughters would be in the safety of her arms.

She would spend only one full day in Panama and then turn them all around to head for home. Time was of the essence, as Henry indicated, so she would waste no time on visiting. The girls were all that mattered. Henry's reticence regarding the sudden collapse of his and Violet's marriage was concerning. She feared there was considerably more to the story than his letter indicated. She only hoped that it was not scandalous enough to affect the entire family. The girls were innocents in this predicament.

∞

Jane was savoring a calming cup of chai between tasks when her husband tromped into the living room, smelling of burnt cane from the mill. "Are you all packed, my love? Do you need me to help you in any way?" John offered.

She shook her head. "I don't need much for this short a trip. I'll be in and out in a matter of days. Henry knows exactly when I will be arriving and has arranged to pick me up from the port."

"Have you told our girls you are going?"

"Yes, I spoke to them both. Come and relax a bit. You've been working so hard lately I've barely seen you."

"Don't worry about me." John took a few steps toward her when suddenly his balance faltered.

Jane rushed to his side and grabbed his upper arm to steady him. He looked at her dizzily. "What's going on? Are you all right?"

"No, I'm okay. I just need to sit for a minute." John's breathing was labored and shallow.

She thought of his days ahead without her. "I'm not taking any chances. I'm sending for the doctor."

Dr. Kumar strode through the door with his stethoscope around his neck and swung his medical bag onto the nearest chair in one fluid motion. Jane stepped back out of his way as he inserted the earpieces of his stethoscope to examine John.

"His breathing is a bit labored. I want him checked out at the hospital. He'll need to get a few tests to confirm what's going on. He's likely overcome with exhaustion from overdoing things at work, but I don't want to take any chances," Dr. Kumar pronounced. "Let's get him transported immediately. You can both ride along with me. I can brief the cardiologist at the hospital."

Jane nodded her agreement and helped Dr. Kumar get John loaded into the doctor's wagon.

At Kingstown General, the cardiologist confirmed that John had had a mild heart attack.

"I'm prescribing aspirin and bed rest for two weeks. He shouldn't be lifting anything or doing anything but lying down. Can you ensure that he will comply with these orders?" The doctor's eyes bypassed John and looked at Jane.

"Yes, doctor, I'll make certain he—"

"What, are you kidding me? I can't leave the sugar mill for two weeks." John's voice creaked.

Jane and the cardiologist both fixed him with a serious stare. "This is serious, Mr. Simons. If you don't rest, you could bring on another heart attack, and *that* one could be fatal," the doctor warned. "You want to stay alive, don't you?"

John sighed and nodded in assent.

Two hours later, Jane had him home and settled comfortably in their bedroom with a bowl of his favorite soup on a tray, the newspaper folded on the side. She'd been thinking the whole time she'd been cooking and come to the only logical conclusion.

"I'm not leaving you," she declared, settling into the chair at his bedside. "I'll have to ask Mahala to go instead."

"I—I'm not going to fight with you, my love. It wouldn't do me any good anyway, would it?"

"No, it wouldn't." Her mouth curved up in a small smile, just as Mahala and Kavita arrived to check on them.

"How are you feeling, Papa?" Mahala asked, bending over to kiss him.

"Much better, now that you're here." He gave her a weak smile. "They said I had a heart attack, and they want to prevent me from having another one."

"You need to take this seriously, Papa. You'll have to follow the doctor's orders." She pulled up the blanket a little higher on his chest.

When John started to doze off, Jane motioned to Mahala and Kavita to follow her out to the living room.

"Obviously I can't leave him in this condition," she sighed. "Mahala, would you go to Panama to get Henry's girls, instead of me?"

"Henry gets what he wants, doesn't he?" Mahala muttered.

"I can see if one of the neighbor's boys will go with you, so you will have a male traveling companion," Jane offered.

"Nonsense, I'm a grown woman and I don't need some boy getting underfoot," Mahala said, returning her mother's gaze. Jane stiffened at her raised voice.

"I know, sweetheart, but it is customary for a woman of your age to have a man accompany her." Jane swiveled her head. "Kavita, tell her."

Kavita opened her mouth, agreement written on her face—then paused. Jane watched her expression soften. "Once Mahala knows she can accomplish something, it would take the full force of an eruption from Soufrière to stop her. I think . . . she can handle herself. She's both confident and capable, my daughter." Kavita mused, delight now evident in her countenance. "Plus, she's going to have two children to shepherd home—and you know how boys can be. She doesn't need another child to tote around."

"You're probably right," Jane conceded.

"I can do this." Mahala reached out and took Jane in a warm embrace. "Papa's going to be okay. He has to be."

CHAPTER 15
Mahala

THE FOLLOWING MORNING, MAHALA HURRIEDLY got ready for her trip, shoving some clothes into her leather case. Normally she would take care to fold each item expertly to prevent any wrinkling, but Jane had told her time was of the essence. She tossed in minimal toiletries and makeup in a small compartment on the top of the valise.

Before closing the case, it occurred to her that she should include a small gift for each of her nieces. She searched the contents of her room and decided on a pair of blue silk hair ribbons for Sofia and a wooden hair clip and stick for Lily. Both would complement their luminous black hair beautifully. She found a small cloth to wrap them in and tucked them both into the corner of her valise.

Mahala had some trepidation about her mission. She loved her brother and wanted to lend her support, but she also had some uneasiness about why he was in this situation. As much as she loved him, she knew he could be domineering and controlling. She had felt his wrath on a number of occasions when his desires were met with resistance. Perhaps it might be good for his daughters to have a short break from the tension of their home, but Mahala didn't think it was fair to separate them from their own mother for long.

From her own brief experiences with her sister-in-law, Mahala understood Violet to be a sweet, polite woman who easily bent to her husband's will. She abhorred conflict and would do anything to avoid it. She loved her girls intensely, so it was difficult to imagine that she would part with them willingly. Mahala's thoughts swirled with the possibilities of what could have happened. She wasn't sure she was willing to press her brother for an explanation, but she was curious about how the situation had become so dire.

With John convalescing, Jane and Kavita accompanied her down to the port in Kingstown and bid her bon voyage.

Mahala was fashionably outfitted in a light green, long-sleeved dress with a snug band at her waistline secured with a large fabric-covered button. The full skirt reached down to her mid-calf. Her long hair was gathered into a bun under a rounded sun hat adorned with a thin band of dark green ribbon tied into a bow on the side of the narrow brim. She looked the picture of island elegance.

She checked her purse for the last time to make sure she had her tickets and traveling documents. Kavita stepped close, kissed her cheek, and wrapped her in a tight squeeze. "I put a little surprise in your valise for you to open later when you get settled in your cabin. Safe travels, my dear daughter. I love you."

"Thanks, Mai, but you didn't have to do that."

"Oh, hush now, I wanted to do something nice for you."

Jane moved closer to the pair and said, "Take care of yourself, Mahala. Stay out of trouble. There are disreputable men who might try to take advantage of a woman traveling alone."

"I'll be fine, I promise." She smiled. "I know how to guard my reputation. If I encounter a scoundrel, I'll clobber him with my purse! And if that doesn't work, I'll get the ship's security detail involved."

Jane frowned. "Don't joke like that. This is a serious matter."

"I know, Mama. I'll be careful. I love you both. I'll be back in less than a week with two adorable little girls in tow," Mahala exclaimed. She grabbed her valise in one hand and waved goodbye to Jane and Kavita with the other as she headed up the gangway.

Mahala had a small meal on the ferry before arriving in Barbados, where she boarded a much larger ocean liner bound for Panama. Clutching her bag, she wandered down the hall in the direction a porter had pointed, until she came to her cabin door.

"Hello?" she said, letting herself in. The shared cabin was small but efficiently laid out with two built-in bunk beds and a small washstand stocked with a basin, fluffy white towels, and soap. A small wooden bench stood opposite, its back attached directly to the wall and its thin seat cushion upholstered in a floral pattern. As she stepped inside, she realized every piece of furniture was either nailed down to the floor or attached to the nearest wall to prevent it from sliding away as the ship rocked through the inevitable swells of the ocean.

"Hello," a tall, thin woman replied from the port hole. "You must be Miss Simons. I'm Miss Woodford—um, Cynthia, I mean," she stammered. "Please call me Cynthia." Mahala's cabinmate had mounds of chestnut-brown curls piled high on her head. A few wispy tendrils dangled loose at the back of her neck, which Cynthia kept nervously attempting to smooth back into her coiffure.

"Pleased to meet you, Cynthia. I'm Mahala," she said as she reached to shake hands. "Would you like the top bunk or bottom?"

On the first night of her sea voyage, Mahala dined with her newly made acquaintance. They were seated at a table with two couples who seemed to be quite familiar with each other, as they were already engrossed in conversation when Mahala and Cynthia arrived. Without missing a beat in the discussion, the couples both politely looked up, nodded, and smiled a greeting to the two young girls. The girls returned their smiles and took their seats.

The steward placed the first course of consommé in front of each person and returned with beverages for everyone. The girls chatted while dinner was being served. Mahala learned that Panama City was Cynthia's home, which she was returning to after an extended visit with relatives in Barbados. Soon she would be reunited with her fiancé who, as Mahala discovered, was a medical doctor in the same hospital as Henry.

"I bet they are friends, or at least have come across each other at the hospital from time to time," Mahala remarked. "When are you getting married?"

"Just three months from now!" said Cynthia, beaming.

"Congratulations! You must be ecstatic. Have you known him for long?"

Cynthia's eyes sparkled as she smiled. "Actually, I've known him all my life. We grew up next door to each other and were betrothed from the time we were babies. Our families are very close—he's an amazing man. I'm very lucky to have such a match, but the best part about it is that I've always loved him." Just then their server arrived with light, flaky coconut biscuits and steaming cups of tea. Mahala's mouth watered with anticipation.

"That's wonderful," she said. "You're fortunate that the man your family picked was the man you wanted anyway. I wish I were as lucky."

"Oh, I'm sorry." Cynthia sipped her cup of tea.

"It's—it's okay." She brushed a few crumbs off her lap and smoothed her dress. For a moment, the silence was awkward, but she was glad Cynthia didn't pry.

"Your dress is beautiful," her companion finally said. "Did you have it made on St. Vincent?"

"I made it myself," Mahala declared.

"You're so talented!"

"I like you, my friend!" Mahala announced with a broad smile on her face. "You're a master at changing subjects! Come on, let's go to the cigar lounge for an after-dinner drink and have some fun." She stood and pulled Cynthia by her arm toward the door.

"We can't go in there. It's for gentlemen only."

"Wanna bet? Follow my lead," Mahala said. "We paid just as much as the men! Let them throw us out."

They waltzed through the entrance with purpose, registering the attendant's stare sweeping over them as they took a seat at the bar. The bartender tipped his head and betrayed a sly smile as he continued stirring a long-handled silver spoon in a cocktail glass. Mahala quickly had him wrapped around her little finger. She complimented him and talked her way into drinks for the two of them. It was only after several other male passengers complained that the young ladies were asked to leave. As she dozed off to the rocking of the ship, Mahala still smiled over her small victory—gaining entry to the exclusive lounge in the first place.

When the ship docked at the port, Mahala and Cynthia disembarked along with the other passengers cascading down the long gangway. The steep angle was hard for Mahala to navigate in heels, but she managed to maintain her poise. When they reached the dock at the bottom, the young women set their small valises down and embraced each other with tears filling their eyes. They made a promise to stay in touch and wished one another the best of luck for the near future. Cynthia's parents waved to her, and she dashed away.

Mahala scanned the crowd for her brother and spotted him almost immediately. At his height he stood out among the rest of the people gathered on the dock. He'd arrived dressed in a light gray suit with a blue pinstripe tie and a Panama hat. The caramel skin of his face was smooth and glowing from a recent fresh shave.

"How was the journey, little sister?" Henry asked as he hugged Mahala and relieved her of her valise. He guided her toward his car and loaded her things into the trunk.

"It was actually quite nice. My cabinmate was a dear—you may know her fiancé, actually. He works at the same hospital you do. I forget his name, but I wrote it down . . ." She trailed off, noticing Henry's eyes darting around, almost as if he was expecting someone to pop out from hiding, Mahala thought.

"Watch yourself!" He pulled her to his side, avoiding a collision with another pedestrian. Mahala was awestruck with the frenetic activity of the port. It was nothing like what she knew on St. Vincent. This place was teeming with people racing over pavement, shouting, waving, and whistle blowing. She wondered if all of Colon was this busy.

Mahala felt proud of herself for making the journey successfully on her own. Her confidence had not been misplaced. Now, she was determined to take in as much as she could of Panama in her limited time here.

CHAPTER 16
Henry

Colon, Panama

As he drove, Henry's thoughts raced between explanations, excuses, and strategies for getting out of the marital crisis that would affect his young family's lives. He'd tried desperately to fix things with Violet, but she would not relent. In their fight two months ago, she'd threatened to poison the children against him for what he had done to her, for destroying their happiness over a cheap infidelity. Admittedly, his latest affair had been different from the others. He could actually see himself starting a new life with Carolina.

That was when Henry had started preparing himself for the end of his marriage. He'd known he would have to act swiftly if he wanted to ensure that Sofia and Lily were brought up the way *he* wanted them to be. His first thought was to send them to St. Vincent.

Jane was getting older, but he was sure that she would welcome the chance to spend more time with her granddaughters. He knew from experience that his mother was powerless to refuse his requests when he was in need of her help—and he had no intention of allowing Violet to keep the girls from him.

Divorce was not something to be proud of, he knew. He would have to be careful to keep the damage to his reputation minimal. That meant keeping both Violet and the girls out of Colon for the time being. Luckily, Violet was currently away visiting her sister for a few days. She was far enough from the city not to get wind of what he was planning. Still, he had to move quickly before her return.

Mahala shifted in the seat next to him, floating a hand out the window to play with the breeze. As he took a few more turns, his mind drifted back to happier days at the start of his relationship with his wife. He was just twenty years old and had never been in love before. When he first met Violet, he was enraptured by her striking beauty and voluptuous figure. Henry fell instantly, madly in love with her, and it was evident to him that she returned his feelings.

Given that they were so drawn to each other—and her father was delighted to welcome a soon-to-be doctor as a son-in-law—they decided to marry quickly. Sofia was born nine months to the day after the wedding, and Lily arrived two years later. As Henry graduated into hospital work, he could admit he'd had little time to nurture the relationships with his wife and children. He still loved Violet . . . but in recent years, his attention *had* begun to stray. Henry had always returned to her, and she welcomed him back without questioning his loyalty—or so he'd thought. However, this last time was different. Violet seemed unable to get over his latest dalliance. She told him in no uncertain terms that she could no longer tolerate his betrayals.

He remembered the confrontation they had had just several weeks ago.

The clock was still chiming its midnight bells when Henry creaked the door open slowly and slipped into his house. He removed his hat and placed it on the hat rack, shrugged out of his jacket and hung it on the hook, making as little noise as possible. He tiptoed into the kitchen and was startled to see Violet sitting at the table, drinking a cup of tea.

"I didn't expect you to still be awake at this hour." He slowly approached her and reached a hand out, touching her gently on the shoulder. Her body was stiff and unmoving, but she did not reject his attempt to kiss her softly on the cheek. She swirled her tea, replaced her cup into its saucer, and watched the tea leaves gently settle to the bottom.

"Your hours are getting increasingly late," Violet stated, raising one eyebrow. "What was it this time that kept you?" Her voice was eerily calm, its tone flat and even. "You know what, don't bother. I don't have the energy to listen to your excuses tonight."

"Sweetheart, what's wrong? You know I usually have evening house calls after my regular office hours and then I have to chart afterwards. I would come home earlier but I find it easier to finish up at my office. I have everything I need there at my fingertips," Henry explained.

She looked up at him, and he was taken aback to find her eyes shining with tears. "I can't do this anymore. I thought I could live this way, but it's destroying me. I love you and I love the family that we've made together, but I don't deserve to be treated this way. I know you've been unfaithful to me." Henry felt his heart sink. "And the sad part is that I've known for some time and I haven't had the courage to confront you. As strange as it sounds, I thought you might work it out of your system. We were young when we got married . . ." She trailed off, then cleared her throat. "I'm leaving you, Henry. I'm taking the girls with me. You don't deserve our love. Go love your new toy. I'm sure it'll take her some time to figure out who you really are. I wish I could say that I pity her, but I really pity you. You slice through life like a sharp knife, never pausing when you make others bleed."

Henry stood still, trying to come up with a response that would assuage Violet. He did love her, but he also loved Carolina. Over the years, he had always managed to compartmentalize his affairs. The other women had just been playthings for him, but not Carolina. She was real, she was beautiful, she was exciting, and most of all she didn't put demands on him. She was satisfied with the stolen moments that they had together. It was Henry who had changed. He had begun to fall in love with her.

"I'm not the first man to have strayed outside of marriage. You know this doesn't mean anything to me." Even as he said the words, he knew they were a lie. He was trying to buy some time so he could figure out a way that he could still have them both. "Just think of the girls. How will you take care of them without any income?"

"I'll figure something out. I just can't ignore this anymore." She stood, turned, and walked out of the room.

Henry remained in the kitchen until he was sure she was asleep. He knew he could not allow Violet to dictate the course of his life, of his children's lives. He started to formulate his plan. He knew he could depend on his mother's support to solve this problem.

Henry was snapped back to the present as he rolled into the driveway that he shared with his neighbor, Mrs. Garcia. Having one's own car was an uncommon luxury in Colon. It was a testament to his success that Henry was one of the few to be able to afford one.

Mahala peered through the car window with her eyes wide. Henry could see her straining to get a first look at her nieces before she got out. He spotted their heads as they popped up from the large picture window. Mrs. Garcia had agreed to watch the girls for Henry as she had done occasionally when Violet asked her.

Henry got out of the car and rounded the passenger's side to open the door for his sister. As Mahala stepped out of his grand automobile, a woman strolled by the back of the car with her baby comfortably nestled in a pretty wicker carriage. The sun glinted off the highly polished metal wheels of the pram, the baby safely ensconced under the large sateen parasol. This—the safety, the luxury, the decorum—was exactly why Henry chose to settle his family here. And now Violet was trying to destroy that.

The little girls spilled out onto the driveway from the majestic front door with Mrs. Garcia behind them. Henry didn't bother trying to scoop up his daughters when their favorite aunt was present. He allowed them to run right past him into Mahala's loving open arms.

"Aunt Mahala! We haven't seen you in forever!" Sofia leaped upon her. Lily clung to her aunt's dress, tugging it until she was picked up. At five years old, Lily was still as light as a feather.

"Sweet girl, come, let me love you up." She gathered both girls into her arms simultaneously, marveling at how much they had grown since she last saw them. "Sofia, you simply must tell me everything about the second grade," Mahala purred softly, giving her a kiss and a squeeze.

"Oh, Aunt Mahala, you already know about the second grade," Sofia giggled as both girls slid down from their aunt's grasp. "Come on, I want to show you my new doll. Her name is Gertrude." Sofia grabbed Mahala's hand and proceeded to pull her up the walkway.

"What a sophisticated name for a doll. I simply must meet her at once." Mahala reached out her free hand to Lily and happily added her to Sofia's convoy into the house. Anyone looking at this scene would have assumed that the girls were Mahala's from the striking family resemblance and gleaming ebony hair that they all shared.

Henry thanked his neighbor for watching his daughters and followed the procession inside, bringing along Mahala's valise. He quickly scanned the neighborhood for anyone unexpected or out of place. He suspected that Violet might want to keep an eye on his movements while she was visiting her sister in Panama City. He didn't want her knowing that Mahala was in town for fear she might suspect what he was planning to do with the girls. He knew what he was about to do would not be easy for his daughters, but he was driven by his overwhelming need to control not only his own, but his family's destiny.

Henry had explained that they were going to see their grandparents in St. Vincent, but he did not tell them that they wouldn't be returning to Panama nor that he would no longer be living with their mother. He told himself they were too young to truly understand what was happening.

When the girls were settled, playing with their toys, Henry looked up at Mahala. "You know you took a big risk—a young woman alone, vulnerable, without the protection of a man," Henry scolded in a hushed tone. "Look, you're doing me a great favor here so I'm going to overlook it, but you should know I don't approve."

"Nothing happened. I guess I'm more capable than you give me credit for," she hissed back at him.

CHAPTER 17
Mahala

It was early in the morning before breakfast, but Mahala could already hear the soft voices of her nieces playing outside her bedroom. When she walked into the living room, she saw Lily trotting her little toy wooden horses around the floor, making them prance and jump over the protruding claw-foot legs of the side table. She leaped her favorite midnight-colored stallion from the polished hardwood to the wool rug as if across a large puddle. Each time she made her horses jump higher, her eyes sparkled, and she giggled louder. Meanwhile, Sofia was feeding Gertrude her pretend breakfast and gently wiping her mouth with a cloth napkin.

Mahala knelt on the floor and joined them, trying to act as though her visit did not have the life-altering consequences that only she and Henry knew of. Her stomach rumbled. "I'm starting to get hungry—is anyone else ready for some real breakfast?"

"We are!" the girls cried in unison.

"Okay, but before that, I have a little surprise for both of you. Come, follow me." She led them into the guest bedroom, found her valise, and searched for where she'd tucked the small cloth bundle containing her two gifts. She set it on the bed behind her. "Come see what it is."

Mahala patted the bed. “Sit over here, nice and close, and let me love you up a little first.” After she snuggled with her nieces, she reached behind her and grasped the gifts, one in each hand, and made a closed fist to draw out the suspense. When she could see the girls’ eyes widen with anticipation she opened her right hand, which held the pair of blue silk hair ribbons for Sofia, and then the left, which held the wooden hair clip and stick for Lily. Both girls screamed with delight.

“Oh, Aunt Mahala, I love them!” Sofia exclaimed. She bounded off the bed and ran out of the room. “I’m going to show Gertrude how nice these ribbons are!”

Lily gave her aunt a hug. “Aunt Mahala, will you put the clip in my hair?”

“You mean right now?”

“Yes, I want to look like you!”

“Okay, come here and let me smooth your hair back,” she said as she gathered three equal plaits from the top half of her head, twisted them, and pulled them up to the center of the back of the child’s head. She positioned the clip over the mass of thick hair and then gently inserted the wooden pick sideways to secure it. “You look like a little doll. Speaking of dolls, let’s see where your sister and Gertrude are, so I can get some breakfast started for us.” She swept out of her room, her heart filling with pride for these two young girls. She found Sofia around the corner in the living room on the floor with her new doll. “What’s Gertrude’s favorite breakfast, Sofia?” she asked as she flipped her thick ebony braid behind her shoulder.

“She loves farine porridge just like Grandma Jane makes!”

“Well, she’s in luck because I know just how to make that. Grandma Jane taught me how when I was just about your age.” She grabbed the pot and assembled the ingredients she needed and let Sofia add the sweet milk and cinnamon, just like her mother did for her when she was that age.

CHAPTER 18
Mahala

MAHALA WOKE ON HER FINAL morning in Colon, her head filled with last-minute tasks to get the girls ready for their journey to St. Vincent. She'd expressed her concern to Henry the night before about taking the girls without Violet's knowledge, but he had assured her that he had things under control. She could see his thoughts turning behind his eyes as he sat silently and stoically in his chair. She knew better than to challenge him about running his own family.

She grabbed her robe and wrapped it tightly around her as she walked into the kitchen and saw Henry and the girls preparing breakfast. The sunny-side up eggs were sizzling in one frying pan while the bacon was popping and splattering in another. "Mmmm, that smells delicious." Mahala, determined to help, reached into the cupboard, took out the plates, and set them on the table. Violet was the cook of the family, but Henry did a decent job with breakfast, especially if it was bacon and eggs. He never attempted anything more complicated as far as Mahala knew. "What else can I do to help?" she asked.

"You can toast the bread." Henry motioned to the plate with several slices of bread stacked up like a tower.

Mahala plucked two slices of bread off the plate and slid them into the two metal basket swingers on either side of the exposed electric coils. It took less than a minute for each side to toast before she had to flip it over for the other side. "I love this machine," Mahala marveled. "We still toast bread in the oven at home."

"I know. I'm a little afraid of it," Henry said, chuckling.

Sofia chimed in, "I'll get the silverware, Aunt Mahala! We can be a team!" She pulled out the drawer so fast, everything slid to the front and banged against the edge of the drawer with a clank. Mahala stepped closer to help her niece.

When breakfast was over and the dishes cleared, Henry turned to Mahala, and the two exchanged a knowing look without words. Mahala's stomach flipped, imagining the nerves Henry was feeling about saying goodbye to his daughters.

Henry gathered Sofia and Lily tight to his chest and kissed them both on the cheek. "You know I love you girls more than anything else in the world." His words sounded tight in his throat.

"We know, Papa," Sofia said, beaming. "Why isn't Mama coming with us this time?"

Mahala held her breath. This was the second time this question had come up. Sofia had asked last night, too, when Mahala helped Henry get the girls ready for bed.

"As I told you last night, Mama is helping your other aunt with something really important, so she can't get away right now, love."

"But Papa, we've never gone without Mama," Sofia protested.

"I know, I know, but don't worry, Aunt Mahala will take really good care of you. You'll see, everything is going to be just fine." Henry made eye contact with his sister and lowered his voice. "Mahala, you keep my girls safe and send a telegram as soon as you arrive in St. Vincent. I won't be able to rest until I know that you have arrived safely."

"I'll guard these girls with my own life. I would never let anything happen to them," Mahala assured him. "They are packed and ready to go. I have the tickets you arranged for us all. I'll send a telegram the instant we arrive in St. Vincent. Don't worry about a thing."

Mahala bid her brother farewell as he reluctantly left for the hospital. Guilt weighing like a stone in her stomach for the part she was playing in deceiving Violet, she hoped that her brother and sister-in-law could work out an arrangement that was acceptable for them both, but at the same time she feared Henry's ruthless nature would leave Violet at a loss. As she well knew, her brother's will would always prevail, no matter whose feelings got in the way.

A short while after Henry left for work, Mahala gathered the girls' trunks with her own small valise and called a taxi service to bring them to the port in Colon. They arrived early and had some time to kill before the departure, so Mahala allowed them to walk along the port and go into the market along the canal area. They found a shop that sold various toys and sundries, including a unique collection of wooden horses. Lily was drawn like a magnet to the display, captivated by the abundant selection of stallions and mares. Meanwhile, Sofia proceeded further into the shop out of sight—until Mahala heard her shout, "Aunt Mahala, please can I get a traveling outfit for Gertrude? It's a shame that we are traveling in such elegant dresses, and she has her tired old lace frock."

Mahala glanced over at Lily, who still seemed enthralled with the horses. "Lily, are you okay up here? Sofia needs my help with picking out a new dress for her doll." Mahala scanned the store. A shopkeeper walked past her, straightening shelves and propping the door open to allow some fresh air to circulate. "Be a good girl and stay right here, so I can find you. Okay?" Lily nodded absently and Mahala called, "I'm coming, love. Yes, you can get a new dress for Gertrude."

As she approached the back of the shop, the clerk at the checkout counter was chatting with Sofia. "What a beautiful porcelain face she has, just like a princess. She must be very special to you. Her auburn locks are combed so neatly. Did you style her yourself?"

"Yes, I make sure to keep her hair smooth just like mine. My mama taught me how important it is to be presentable when we go out. Papa likes us to look very pretty too, because everyone knows that we are Dr. Henry Simons's family," Sofia smiled.

Mahala caressed the top of her niece's head and let her hand slide down the back of her hair to the nape of her neck. When she heard Sofia's description, she was embarrassed. She knew Henry guarded his reputation and status as a medical doctor above almost anything else. Appearances had to be always maintained. It was sad—no, maybe *merciful*, Mahala thought—that Sofia hadn't yet figured out her father's manipulation and control.

"Lily? Did you select something? It's time to be on our way." Mahala headed toward the front of the shop. They had an hour until the ship's departure, but she didn't want to cut it too close. But when she reached the horse display, Lily was not there. Mahala darted around the store, checking every corner, and then realized that the door was propped open. She approached the salesclerk on the floor. "Have you seen my little niece, about five years old, with ebony hair pulled back into a clip, dressed in a yellow paisley dress?" Mahala implored.

"I saw her a few minutes ago before I went to the back storeroom, but when I returned, she wasn't there," the clerk answered with a shrug.

"I told her not to move, but she must have slipped out. I need to find her right away! We're supposed to board a steam ship in less than an hour!" blurted Mahala. "If something has happened to her, I'll never forgive myself!"

Mahala dropped the doll clothes at the register, grabbed Sofia's hand, and bolted out of the store. "Where could she have gone?" If someone had taken Lily, she might never find her again. Henry would never forgive her—and worse yet, she would never forgive herself.

Mahala frantically inquired with every shopkeeper and pedestrian she came across. It was now noon, and the sun was searing into them. They had a half hour before the ship departed and still no Lily in sight. Mahala was drenched in sweat, exhausted with the dreadful possibilities turning over in her head. How could she face Henry again? What would Violet say, her child stolen from her not once, but twice—or forever?

Just then, Sofia gasped and pointed straight at the scene across the street, where a unique horse tricycle was pulled up near the public fountain in the square. Beside it, Mahala could see a mother and her two small children. Just then, Lily came into focus. She was standing between the fountain's edge and the horse, stroking the sleek coat of the gleaming wooden steed, her eyes steady with pure awe. "There she is, Aunt Mahala!" Sofia cried. "She's in front of the fountain!"

"Oh, thank God in heaven above!" Mahala dashed over to the family and didn't have to say much in explanation. Her blouse clung to her body, saturated in perspiration. Her once perfectly coiffed hair had loosened, leaving several frayed ends sticking out. It was obvious by both the distress and relief Mahala wore on her face that she was the missing aunt.

"Lily! I specifically told you not to move from where you were! What were you thinking?" Mahala chastised her young niece.

"I'm sorry, I couldn't help it. I saw this handsome beast outside, and I just had to pet him."

"I can see that, love." Mahala reached down and clasped the child's small hand in her own. "I know how much you love horses, and this is an admirable creature. You're very lucky that this nice family allowed you to see him."

She smiled and sighed in relief—which did not last more than a brief moment as she looked down at her watch and saw they had just fifteen minutes before the ship departed. She grabbed her two nieces by the hand, thanked the woman profusely, and set off for the port at a gallop worthy of a stallion. They still had a chance of making it, but it would be very close. They would have to count on the good graces of the harbormaster to let them through quickly. Mahala had all the passports as well as her tickets for the ship safely tucked into her pocketbook. She prayed silently, dragging the girls along. She didn't know how she would explain it to Henry if she missed it and failed him.

She saw the ship in sight—they hadn't closed the gangway yet. She slung Lily up on her right hip and grabbed Sofia's hand with her left, hoping she could reach for her pocketbook without dropping Lily. She trudged up the steep incline and managed to hand the tickets and passports to the ship's agent.

"We made it!" Sofia and Lily cheered in unison.

"We certainly did!" Mahala agreed, gasping for breath. "I think we deserve to celebrate! My friend Ruby, in New York, told me about a sweet bubbly new drink called an ice cream soda that's all the rage in America. Let's see if we can ask someone to make it for us."

CHAPTER 19
Mahala

St. Vincent, British West Indies

MAHALA HADN'T ANTICIPATED HOW DIFFICULT it would be to keep two small girls in control and out of danger for three days aboard an ocean liner. She had a renewed sense of respect for what Violet must do daily. Despite some minor mishaps, she did manage to arrive home safely with her two nieces in tow.

John met her at the port in Kingstown. When Sofia and Lily saw their grandfather, they squealed with glee and bolted over to him, launching themselves into his arms simultaneously. John staggered back a step, attempting to remain upright and hold on to his granddaughters.

"My precious little darlings! You have grown a foot since I've seen you last! What's your mother feeding you?" He lavished them with kisses and hugs and placed them back on the ground. Righting his hat firmly back on his head, he waved a hand to the ship's porter to identify his daughter's luggage. He walked with his granddaughters, Mahala trailing behind them. "Papa, what are you doing here? You're supposed to be resting at home. Why didn't you send someone else to get us?"

"I've had enough rest. I'm just about crawling out of my own skin. I've never been fussed over so much in my entire life. I had to get out of there. Honestly, I've gotten most of my strength back already," John said.

"Grandpa, you'll never believe how much fun we had on the ship," Sofia exclaimed. "We listened to the band playing music, we looked for stars from the promenade deck, we ate until our tummies felt like bursting. We even had a special treat called an ice cream soda. Aunt Mahala told them how to make it, and it was the most fizzy, sweet, chocolate thing I ever tasted. You can get it in other flavors, but chocolate is my favorite. It felt like it was exploding in my mouth!" Her brown eyes were opened wide as she related the story to her grandfather.

"It sounds like you had a wonderful trip." John called a porter to load the girls' two trunks and Mahala's small valise onto his wagon. The man secured them tightly with the long leather straps, then helped Mahala up to the seat first, then lifted each of the girls up to her. John tipped him handsomely for his much-needed service. Finally, John jumped in, grabbed the leather reins, and encouraged the horses to move with a quick flick of his wrists. Mahala felt the balmy island breeze blow across her face as John drove the pair of mares in the uncovered wagon. The familiar call of the birds and the whoosh of the waves rushing up the sandy beach were comforting sounds to her.

"Did everything go all right in Panama?" John asked, eyes fixed on the road.

"I'm not sure I would say that," Mahala answered, also looking straight ahead but lifting both eyebrows. "We encountered a few problems, but we're here in one piece and that's all that matters now."

"It's so good to see my little ones," John said, beaming.

When they arrived at the Simons house, Jane ran out to meet the wagon. John secured the horses and the girls jumped down to the ground, where Jane wrapped her arms around both of them and squeezed tight. "It's so good to see you, my sweethearts! Come, let's get you settled, and you can tell me all about your trip." She flashed a smile to Mahala and then ushered them into the house. "You can use your father's old bedroom. I put a few of your aunt's dolls and stuffed animals in there so that it looks more like a little girls' room now. It's cozy, but you should both be comfortable in there together."

As the girls snacked greedily on Jane's special rice pudding, Mahala filled Jane and John in on what little she knew. It wasn't clear to any of them if Sofia and Lily's stay was temporary or permanent. Mahala had no doubt that Jane and John would do their best to make them feel welcome and wanted until they heard more from Henry on what his plan was for the future.

When the girls were settled, Mahala said goodbye to her nieces and walked back over to her own house. She was looking forward to seeing her mother but felt anxiety creeping up her spine. She needed to get back to her plans for her own future—a future she knew Henry wouldn't approve of. Even from fourteen hundred miles away, she was not safe from her brother's influence. Mahala knew Henry had passed along to John possible candidates for her to marry. She had come across more than a few telegrams John had carelessly left visible on the kitchen table. The nerve of Henry. She had to figure out a way to thwart his attempt to dominate her life.

CHAPTER 20

Jane

Jane looked up when Mahala walked into her kitchen. "What are you doing for the next hour?" she asked.

"Why? Do you need help with something, Mama?" Mahala approached and carved a slice of fresh banana bread, tore off a corner, and popped it in her mouth.

"Honestly, I just need a bit of a break. Would you mind entertaining Sofia and Lily for a while?" She smiled sweetly as she handed Mahala a napkin.

"You can have two hours if that helps. I'll take them to the beach."

Jane's shoulders loosened as her mind flooded with relief. "Oh, sweetness, that's wonderful. I'll pack a beach bag for them." She started to get up.

"You sit there. I'll take care of it." Mahala tossed her napkin on the table as she called out, "Sofia, Lily—we're going to the beach!" Her announcement was immediately met with the sounds of happy shrieks and the clatter of shoes on the steps. Mahala wrapped up several slices of banana bread with a wink and left.

As quiet settled over the house, Jane pulled out two letters: one from Henry, and one from Violet postmarked a few days later, though they'd arrived in the same shipment today. She had shoved them both in her apron pocket when the girls had come into the kitchen earlier. She began to read.

Dear Mama,

I have officially filed for divorce from Violet. I can get one from Mexico without a trial, so I won't have to suffer the embarrassment of a public spectacle.

Enroll the girls in school right away since I don't know when I will be able to bring them back home. Violet will no doubt try to contact you so don't weaken. I don't want her to have the opportunity to steal them from me. She was enraged when she returned home and found the girls missing. She knows the only person I would trust is you. She only wants to make me suffer for my indiscretions.

I won't lie to you, Mama—I've met someone else that I want to start a new life with. I deserve to be happy. This is just temporary. I know you will do the right thing.

Your loving son,
Henry

She set Henry's letter down on top of its envelope and reached for the next one with dread. She almost didn't recognize Violet's handwriting through the scrawled script.

Dear Jane,

I am appealing to you as one mother to another. Please help me bring my girls back home where they belong. They shouldn't be without their mother. I know you love them, but if you have their best interests in mind, you will see that they need to be with me. I loved your son, but he's done some things that I just can't overlook any longer. I'm sure you've suspected what I'm referring to. He's very powerful and is used to getting what he wants. I'm staying with my sister, and I'm trying to get the money together to travel to you. Will you allow me to come? I am heartsick without my babies.
Please, I'm begging you to have compassion. Kiss my girls for me.
Sincerely,
Violet

Jane's body tensed as she folded the letters. Violet was in pain; her granddaughters, despite her and Mahala's efforts, were in pain; yet surely, she owed her loyalty to Henry. She felt torn in half.

Seeking a sympathetic ear, she walked over to see Kavita. Jane spotted her on the side of the house tending her flowers and waved. Kavita set down her gardening tools and waved back. "Are you alone? Where are the girls?" She peeled off her gloves and stuffed them in her apron.

"Mahala took them to the shore." She caught up with Kavita, walking inside behind her. "I—I feel caught in a very bad place." She slid into her usual spot at the table, watching Kavita warm up the tea water and pull out the cups. "I'm doing what Henry asked me to, but I feel sick about how this is tearing the girls up, and Violet." She wrung her hands.

Kavita sat down and rested her hand on Jane's shoulder. "Have you told Henry how you feel?"

"I wrote to him imploring him to work things out with Violet for the children's sake, but all I got in return was this letter." She fished it out of her pocket and waved it in front of Kavita. "And I got one from Violet as well." She held up the second letter. Kavita jumped up, got the tea off the stove, and put it on the table between them. "He's divorcing her, and he's ordered me not to let her see the girls. How can I do that—as a mother?" She registered Kavita's face going slack.

"I don't have the strength to argue with him," Jane admitted. "I don't want to be disloyal to him, but I understand the desperation and heartache that Violet's feeling." Kavita nodded, pushing the sugar bowl and spoon closer to Jane. "Sofia and Lily ask about their mother constantly. They want to know when she's coming to join them for their *visit* at Grandma and Grandpa's house." Jane's heart was breaking for them all.

"Oh, Jane, what an awful situation. Is there anything I can do to help?"

"You're doing it." Her mouth tilted up on one side in a slight smile as she stirred her tea. "Yesterday, both girls broke down into wracking sobs." She took a sip of tea, feeling the warmth as she swallowed. "I'm considering risking Henry's wrath and allowing Violet to see the children."

Kavita was quiet a moment, looking down into her tea. Finally, she squared her shoulders resolutely and grasped Jane's hand. "Girls need their mothers."

That afternoon, while Mahala still had the girls, Jane made her way to the telegraph office and sent a telegram to Violet's sister's house, giving her permission to come and visit. With any luck, Violet would be able to borrow money from her sister for the fare from Panama to St. Vincent. Jane had considered offering to pay for it, but she already felt dangerously close to betrayal. She would have to figure out a way to explain her actions to her son, but right now she felt justified in her decision as a mother. This was the longest that Sofia and Lily had ever been away from home, from Violet. They had been used to visiting St. Vincent for a month at a time, but Violet had always been with them. Jane rushed back home to console the girls and felt mildly better that they would see their mother soon.

The following day, Jane heard a knock on the door and discovered a young boy in a Western Union uniform on her stoop, his bike resting against her house. Her stomach tightened with anticipation. In the telegram, Violet made it clear that she wanted to see the girls desperately but also confirmed that she was no longer authorized to withdraw any funds from their accounts, so she needed time to get the money together to travel to St. Vincent.

Jane inhaled deeply and steeled herself to have another conversation with her grandchildren. Even she was tiring of her own explanations and excuses of why they couldn't see their mother—or father for that matter. She walked back into the living room, telegram clutched in her hand, and found the girls playing dolls.

"Oh, Gertrude, you mustn't fret, your mama loves you so much. She's very busy, but you will see her soon," Sofia consoled her doll. She stroked a hand down Gertrude's long chestnut locks.

Jane blinked back a surge of tears. She bent down to Sofia's side. "Sweetheart, it won't be long now before your mama comes, I promise. She loves you very much, and so does your papa. They know you always have a good time with Grandma and Grandpa. That's why they asked us to take care of you for a while. Don't we have fun?" The girls both peered up at her, looking like lost puppy dogs.

Jane thought fast for a distraction—the paper dolls. "Would you like to see something special?" She dashed into her bedroom, dug through her closet, and pulled out the "rainy day" box she had kept for Mahala to play with as a child. It was filled with Mahala's paper doll collection. She was flooded with memories of how meticulously Mahala would cut out the dolls' clothes, taking pride in dressing them fashionably. She brushed off the cover as she set the box down in front of the girls. Right then, she knew she must wire Violet the money.

On the day of Violet's arrival, Jane dressed Sofia and Lily in their fanciest dresses and expertly combed and plaited their long dark locks. When everyone was ready, John ferried the perfectly coiffed bunch down to the port. Jane could feel the excitement building in her granddaughters by the way they were both tightening their grips on her hands. She looked up to see the passengers streaming down the gangway in a mass exodus from the ship. The crowd started to thin, and the last few passengers trickled out. They were still waiting, but there was no Violet in sight.

"Will you go and see if you can find out where Violet is?" Jane asked.

"Of course, my love." John ambled up the gangway and tried to flag down the porter, but was brushed aside. A few minutes later, she could see another gentleman—his shoulder epaulets filled with more stripes than the first crew member—approach him. She couldn't make out what they were saying from this distance, but watched the man's head shake ominously from side to side.

The girls started to fidget. Jane was growing nervous. She was about to motion to John to come down when he started walking back toward her, a grim look on his face.

"Jane, there's a problem," he whispered. He looked at Sofia and Lily and bent down to their level. "Can I talk to Grandma for a second, sweet things?"

"Where's Mama? Isn't she coming? You said she was on this ship," Sofia demanded.

"I know, sweetie, just let me talk to Grandma Jane for a second." John straightened up and took Jane by the shoulder. He moved her a few steps away from the children. "Violet contracted pneumonia on the ship. It's—it sounds serious. *Very* serious. They called for an ambulance to transport her to the hospital, but it's dire. The doctor on board said"—he took a deep breath—"he said we should prepare the girls."

Jane gasped in horror. "This can't be happening." She felt sick. Beyond John's shoulder, Sofia and Lily waited quietly, sensing something was afoot. Jane cleared her throat and stiffened her spine. "Then we go to the hospital, too. If it's—if there's a chance this is goodbye, we must let them say it."

At the hospital, the girls had cried out with excitement to see Violet, though she'd scarcely been able to lift a hand to pet their cheeks. Jane would never forget the way the awful realization dawned on Sofia's face, even as Lily chattered soothingly that Mama would be better soon.

Violet died the next afternoon. Jane relayed the news to Henry via telegram immediately. His response was short—he was shocked at Violet's untimely death—and while Jane was grateful that he didn't admonish her for making contact with his ex-wife, the reply struck her as suspiciously incomplete. She sent another telegram asking when he would come and take the girls home to Panama again.

The message she received back was not what she expected: Henry was inundated with work, and his new wife had a baby on the way, and he couldn't be expected to leave her. Would she mind terribly holding things together for Sofia and Lily while he sorted things out on his end?

Sorted things out? Jane was not sure what that meant. Her son should come and console his daughters. She felt a flare of anger—he'd taken them from Violet to hoard them, but in her absence, he no longer wanted them? She felt a spike of shame for even entertaining such a dark opinion about Henry, and yet . . . hold things together, she did.

CHAPTER 21

Mahala

Guilt ate at Mahala. For months, she dreamed of Violet—her pale hand lifelessly dangling from the hospital bed only to rise and stroke Sofia's hair; her cold, purple lips kissing Lily's forehead. Sometimes she dreamed she was back on the ship herself, exploring and giggling with Cynthia, only to find it was Violet she was clutching arm in arm.

She awoke from every dream with a cold shiver and a pang of deep, grief-stricken shame. As she lay in the dark, heart rate settling, Mahala would think about her own unique upbringing, the benefits of having two loving mothers, while her poor innocent nieces didn't have a mother at all. And if she hadn't succumbed to Henry's pressure, if she hadn't helped steal his children . . . Violet never would have gotten on that infected ship, never gotten pneumonia, and Sofia and Lily would still have a mother.

Motivated by her guilt, she put her life on hold to help Jane and John provide a loving, supportive home for the girls. She became a second surrogate mother to them, tutoring them in school and serving as their constant companion. Not that Henry was thankful for what she had given up for him. The more she gave, the more he took. She loved her nieces dearly, grateful for the bond they had developed, but her resentment toward Henry was building.

After a sleepless night haunted by not one but two Violet nightmares, Mahala looked at the clock, realizing the girls would have already gone off to school, and walked over to Jane's. She found her in the kitchen cleaning up from breakfast.

"Let me help with that." She gently nudged her over, grabbing the sponge from her, and finished the dishes. Jane sat at the table. "Have you heard anything from Henry lately about taking the girls home to Panama?" She turned looking over her shoulder, drying her hands on the dishtowel.

Jane sighed. "He still doesn't think the time is right. He's afraid that Carolina wouldn't be able to give them the love and attention they deserve." Jane swept her hand over the table, pushing the crumbs to the center. Mahala suspected that Henry himself didn't want any reminders of his failed marriage, nor did he want any friction with his new wife. "I think if Henry wanted custody of his daughters, he would have figured it out by now." Jane pushed her salt and pepper shakers back and forth across the table.

"I'm not going to play governess forever, regardless of the guilt I feel," said Mahala. "I want a life too, and I don't want to have to put Henry's needs above my own. I've done that for far too long." Her face flushed hot.

"Why don't we take Sofia and Lily over to Barbados this weekend? We can visit with some friends and just relax. I think we all deserve it." Jane's mouth turned up into a half smile.

"Don't try to change the subject, Mama. Henry's in the wrong here, and I'm getting tired of it. Something's got to give and it's no longer going to be me." Her voice grew louder.

CHAPTER 22

Kavita

1921

KAVITA CARRIED A WOODEN SERVING tray, laden with refreshments, into the room where John and Jane were seated waiting for her. Light reflected off the tray's smooth polished edges as she placed it on the coffee table in front of them. The glasses on the tray were filled with freshly pressed mango juice with a splash of the island's signature rum and garnished with a sprinkling of lime zest over the top.

"I've invited you here to enlist your help," Kavita began, taking her seat with a sigh. Jane and John exchanged a knowing glance. "I have been looking into possible candidates who would make a suitable husband for Mahala, and I've come up with a list of three men." Kavita handed each of them a glass. "I would like your opinion on each of them and of course if you have any others that you think would do, please speak up. I fear I may have failed her by letting her delay as long as she has," she faltered, taking a sip, "but hopefully it's not too late."

John set his glass down eagerly. "You're right, we can't give up on finding a match for her. It's simply untenable to allow her to relinquish her chance of security because she has the notion that she would be happier to find a man she is in love with on her own. We all know that that could take a long time—she's twenty-one, she has *already* taken a long time—and there is no guarantee that she would be successful."

"Henry knows the Agarwal family," Jane said, spotting one name on Kavita's list. "Their oldest son Jagan is about thirty-five, just the right age for Mahala. He is running his father's shipbuilding business on Barbados, but he returns to St. Vincent often to see his family. Do you want me to ask Henry to find out if he has an intended?"

"That would be great," Kavita answered. "Let's see where we get with his family, and I'll move down the list if necessary." She sniffed. "I'll talk to Mahala before we make any final arrangements. We don't want a repeat of the disaster that happened before."

John ran a hand through his thick hair. "That was an injury to both our families' reputations I didn't think we would heal from. It helped that I suggested another acceptable match for young Mr. Joshi, which both he and the young woman were very pleased with. They already have three children!" he exclaimed.

The following week, Kavita very gingerly broached the subject of marriage with Mahala over breakfast. Breakfast was Mahala's favorite meal of the day; therefore, she was likely to be in a good mood, Kavita thought.

"Darling, I want to talk to you about your future." She dripped the words out of her mouth as slow as honey and waited for Mahala's deep brown eyes to meet hers. Mahala dropped her spoon on the table and looked at Kavita. "Your father and I made a mistake the first time we proposed an arranged marriage for you. You were too young then. But now is the perfect time to secure your future. Henry was kind enough to investigate a young man right in Barbados who is suitable for you. His name is Jagan Agarwal. I want you to consider him." Her eyes pleaded with Mahala. "Most girls your age are either married or, at the very least, engaged."

She watched the panic rise in her daughter's eyes. "Mai, please. Don't you understand that I need to do this for myself? I don't want your help. I don't want Mama and Papa's help either. Tell me you haven't involved them too. Why can't you trust me?" she groaned.

"I do trust you, but not with this. This is something that you need our help on. Won't you just meet the young man we have in mind for you?" Kavita implored.

Mahala's eyes narrowed as she stood abruptly. "I can't discuss this right now, Mai, I'm late for tutoring. Don't do anything!" She scooped up her papers and notebooks, shoved them into her leather bag, and left her mother sitting at the kitchen table, feeling like she had just been through the first round of a prize fight.

CHAPTER 23

Mahala

It was obvious to Mahala that Kavita was not going to give up the idea of an arranged marriage. Mahala experienced a wave of dread that started in the center of her stomach and rose up to her throat. Kavita had likely involved John and Jane in addition to Henry in this newest attempt to get her married. She was not looking forward to the fight she would have on not one, but three fronts at once. As she started to formulate her plan, she realized she would need to enlist Ruby's help.

Mahala Simons
Ratho Mill, St. Vincent VC0274
Dear Ruby,

I'm sorry that it's been a while since my last letter. I wish I had good news to report, but I find myself unhappy. I realized today that soon it will be two years since Violet's death, and two years of Henry saying he will come for his daughters eventually, two years of me picking up the pieces with Mama. I know the girls needed me. I don't begrudge them. After all, if it weren't for me maybe things would've been different. Maybe Violet would have had time to negotiate with Henry, maybe she would have realized his plans, maybe she wouldn't have been on that ship. I could say that I just did what I was asked, that I was serving only as the dutiful sister and daughter yet again. I was, but sometimes I fear I was so eager for my own adventure, so eager to be independent, to get off St. Vincent and see a little more of the world and be my own woman for once, that I let that blind me to my part in all this. My instincts told me this was wrong, and I set those instincts aside for duty and a little taste of freedom. But while I'll carry Violet on my conscience every day, I can't help but think that I've done my time, paid my penance—just a little—with two years of caring for them. Is that a terrible way to think? Where is Henry's guilt, his self-reflection? He was so insistent that we take them from Violet so he could raise them as he saw fit, and yet he's never here. He's happy to let Mama and me take care of them. He's started a new second life while I never got to live my first one. If I don't leave soon, Ruby, that's what my story will be. I'll spend years raising two children who aren't mine until my parents finally wed me to the man of their dreams. Don't think they've forgotten their mission! They've picked out a new suitor they swear is good, or at least good enough, yet again!

My mother says that she has only my best interests at heart, but this can't be true, not if she knows me at all. They couldn't force me into marriage when I was a mere child, and they will not force me into it now. They think they can use fear to manipulate me into doing what they want, threatening to withdraw financial support if I leave St. Vincent. They are betting that I don't have the courage to live without them. I know it will be hard to support myself without their help, but I need to do this, not only to prove them wrong but to prove to myself that I am in control of my own destiny.

Can you speak to your boss and see if he will hire me to be a seamstress? What I'm proposing is frightening, but I feel it's my only option. If I stay in St. Vincent, my family will not relent.

Your loyal friend,
Mahala

Mahala blew on the lightweight airmail paper, attempting to dry the ink so it wouldn't smudge. She folded the letter in three, slipped it into its envelope, and affixed a stamp with King George V's head emblazoned on it, careful not to get the glue on her fingers. She put the letter in her pocketbook and dashed out the door to post the letter immediately. She did not want to waste another minute.

When she got outside, she saw that both the wagon and the cart were already being used so she decided she would ride her bike to the post office in Kingstown. Slinging the strap of her pocketbook across her body, she charged down the road—until she unexpectedly encountered a collection of large, jagged rocks in her path. She tightened her grip on the handlebars, but the bicycle wheels were not able to absorb the shock of the rough terrain, and she was ejected from the seat of the bike up over the handlebars, flying like a blast out of a cannon. She smashed her forehead directly into a thick chunk of volcanic rock and rolled over on her side, utterly dazed. Her vision was blurry; she could feel wetness spreading down her head and over her brow. She lifted her hand to feel the growing bump above her right eye and brought her fingers back into view in front of her face. Bright crimson liquid was smeared on the palm of her hand. She felt lightheaded and faint.

"Are you okay?" a man's voice yelled. Mahala heard the creak of a cart and the clop of hooves somewhere behind her. "I saw you take that bad fall when I was at the top of the hill." There was a pause as the noises stopped—he must have pulled his horse and cart over to the side of the road and tied them up—because a face came into view above her.

"I—I slammed my head into this rock when I fell off my bicycle."

Blood ran in rivulets from the large gash on her forehead. Her palms stung with scrapes and her calves were scratched, her skirt having offered no protection from the craggy ground.

The man gathered her up in his arms awkwardly and hefted her up into the back of the cart. She could feel his leg drag as he carried her. He pushed the small crates containing freshly harvested vegetables back and out of the way to make room for his unplanned passenger. Mahala could not help but think that he was curiously strong for an old man, especially one with a limp.

As he went back to collect her bicycle, pain stabbed across her forehead. "Not too much damage," he said as he wheeled it over. The front tire appeared to have a flat, and the front fender was crunched up from the impact of the crash. He lifted it into the back of his cart beside her, then climbed up to take his seat.

"I'm on my way into Kingstown market. My son has a stall there. I can drop you at the hospital first and then run over to meet him if you don't mind if I just leave you at the door." His face was full of concern and empathy.

"The name's Thomas—Thomas Radcliffe." He flicked the reins, spurring the horse to trot.

"I'm grateful that you came along when you did. I don't know what I would have done without your help." Mahala gently pressed her head in an effort to lessen the pain as the cart bumped along the road.

"I live in Calliaqua just east of here," he explained, turning his head so she could hear him in the back of the cart. Mahala sensed that he was trying to keep her awake by his chatter. She remembered Henry telling her that head injuries could be serious, and it was important to not let someone fall asleep until they could be assessed by a doctor. This man probably feared that she would slip into a coma in the back of his cart. He chattered on. "It's not easy to ride a bicycle on this rocky ground. I've been leading my horse and cart this way for years with a few stumbles myself."

"I know, Mr. Radcliffe. I'm very glad that we chose this particular time to become acquainted," Mahala whispered back to him, as her eyes rolled slowly back, and her lids grew heavy.

"Me too," he answered as he guided the horse and cart along the uneven terrain. "We'll be at the hospital very shortly, so just hang on back there."

They arrived at the hospital, and Mr. Radcliffe managed to get Mahala out of the cart and into the arms of a nearby nurse, who promptly took her vitals and called for a doctor. Thomas vanished in the hustle and bustle before she could thank him again.

"What's your name, miss?" the nurse purred in a soothing voice, pulling the curtain.

"Mahala Simons. I think I'm okay, just—just dazed. It hurts most here . . ." She gingerly touched above her right eye.

"Yes, I can see you must have taken quite a fall. We'll get you all fixed up, don't worry about a thing," the nurse reassured her. She cleaned Mahala's wounds and offered her a cold compress for the contusion while they waited for the doctor. "Do you have any identification with you in case we have to admit you?" Just then Mahala realized that her pocketbook was missing.

"I have identification in my pocketbook, but it's not here," Mahala explained. She must have left it in the back of Mr. Radcliffe's cart. Surely, he would notice her bag when he unloaded his crates. She would have to figure out a way to find him after she left the hospital. For that matter, where was her bicycle? He must've put it somewhere for her, unusable as it was. Her contemplation was interrupted by the doctor's entrance into the exam room.

He took the chart from the nurse and glanced at the information on it. He smiled warmly at Mahala.

"What have we here, young lady?" the doctor said, more of a statement rather than a question. He examined the head wound and thoroughly checked for other injuries over her body. She had minor cuts and bruises on her hands and legs, but otherwise there were no other injuries. He asked the nurse to dim the examination room light and picked up a small lamp. He gently steadied Mahala's head and lifted her eyelids one at a time, passing the light across her eyes. "Dilating appropriately," he noted. She couldn't help but blink painfully. He put his hand up in front of her face with two fingers forming a V. "How many fingers am I holding up, Miss Simons?"

"Two."

"Very good. I see here that you reported blurred vision. Is your vision still blurred, or has it improved?"

"It's still a bit blurred," she admitted.

"On a scale of one to ten, how is your pain?"

"Seven." She exhaled slowly and brought her hand up to the large bump on her head.

"You do have quite a large hematoma on your head. Let's get that fixed up." He motioned to the nurse, who immediately proffered the metal tray laden with a cache of sterile gauze, several rolls of surgical adhesive tape, as well as the requisite bandage scissors. The doctor expertly dressed the wound, taping several layers of gauze in place, snipping the adhesive, and dropping the scissors back on the metal tray with a resounding clang. Mahala winced.

"The pain and swelling should go down in a day or so if you continue to put cold compresses on it. Your vision should return to normal by the end of the day. If not, you should return to get checked out further. Now, who might be able to escort you—?"

Just then, Mr. Radcliffe came around the corner, walking briskly despite his limp, his face flushed. He was clutching her bag in his hand.

"Miss Simons, after I unloaded my crates, I saw this in the cart. When I took a closer look, I realized that it must be yours. I'm sorry I was in such a rush to get to my son's market stall—otherwise, I would have noticed it before I left you here," Thomas said remorsefully.

"Oh, Mr. Radcliffe, you don't have to apologize. I'm just so glad to see you, especially now," she said, relief washing over her. "I have no way of getting back home since my bicycle is not in any shape to be ridden and even if it were, *I'm* not in any shape to ride. Do you think you could take me home to Ratho Mill?"

Mr. Radcliffe must have heard the desperation in her voice. "It would be my pleasure to deliver you home safely. Your family is probably already frantic with worry that you have not returned yet."

This made Mahala think of the letter that she still needed to post.

"Mr. Radcliffe, do you think that we can make a quick stop at the post office first?" she asked, mustering all the energy she had left in her body. Tears pricked at her eyes.

"Of course we can," he said soothingly. "I need to mail some letters for my wife, so it's not out of the way at all."

Thomas carried Mahala out to his cart, this time placing her in the front with him. When he had her secure and as comfortable as he could make her, he climbed up, reached both hands down to pick up the reins, and signaled the horse by flicking his wrists. They arrived at the post office only a few minutes later, though the motion was enough to make Mahala feel she might faint. When she opened her eyes, she found Thomas sneaking a concerned glance in her direction. Her injury was catching up with her now that the adrenaline had worn off.

"Mahala, why don't you give me your letter and just rest here while I run inside to post it along with my own?"

"You're too kind, Mr. Radcliffe, really—it's not necessary for you to go to all that trouble for me."

"Nonsense. It's no trouble at all. You save your strength and I'll be out in a jiffy."

Mahala dug into her bag to retrieve the letter for Ruby and deposited it into Thomas's extended hand. Thomas tucked it in his satchel with a handful of other envelopes—the ones from his wife, she assumed—and left Mahala ensconced in the safety of the sturdy cart. Slinging his bag over his shoulder, he jumped down and tied the horse to the post.

"Thank you, Mr. Radcliffe," Mahala told him before he went in. "I really owe you a debt of gratitude for what you are doing for me."

"I'm pleased to help you. You don't owe me anything." With a smile on his weathered face, he almost skipped into the post office. He took a last look at Mahala before he opened the door to the building. By the time he returned, Mahala was slumped over in the front seat.

"Pop!" A deep voice floated from across the street. "Hang on a minute! You didn't take the cash receipts from the morning." A young man held up the cash box as proof, approaching the side of the cart.

"Oh, sorry, Ben. I guess I was in a hurry to get back to Miss Simons because she left her pocketbook in my cart . . ." He trailed off and shrugged. "Ben, come and meet Miss Simons." He motioned his son closer. "Miss Simons, this is my son Ben. The one I told you about earlier today."

She managed a weak smile. "Oh, yes, pleased to meet you, Mr. Radcliffe." She had no energy in her voice. "You can call me Mahala."

"And please, call me Ben. This old man is 'Mr. Radcliffe.'" He pointed his thumb affectionately toward his father. "It looks like you had quite an accident this morning." His eyes focused on the bandage on her head. "I hope you feel better."

"Thanks," Mahala answered.

"You're in good hands with this guy." He patted his dad on the shoulder. "He'll get you home safe and sound." Ben backed away from his father's cart, giving him room to maneuver.

Mahala appreciated that Mr. Radcliffe drove his cart slow enough to keep the bouncing and jostling to a minimum for her aching head. It was obvious to her that he was a good father and knew how to put others ahead of himself.

As he pulled the cart up to the front of her house, Kavita came barreling out. Thomas lifted her down from the front seat of the cart and gently placed her standing upright.

"Sweetling, whatever happened to you?" Kavita cried.

Mahala saw her mother's eyes move directly to the prominent bandage on her head and then sweep over her body down to her feet. She knew what kind of impression her torn skirt and rumpled dirty blouse would make on her mother. Kavita scooped her into her arms and started to smooth her messy locks with her fingers. "Everything is going to be all right, my sweetling."

"Mai, I'm sorry I caused you to worry. I took my bicycle into town to post a letter and had a rather bad accident. Mr. Radcliffe came to my rescue at just the right time. I'll be fine. It's just some bumps and scrapes that will heal."

"Oh, Mr. Radcliffe, thank you so much. We are indebted to you for your heroic deed," Kavita exclaimed.

"I'm just glad I was a little late getting started this morning, otherwise I might not have found her on the road."

"Thank you again, Mr. Radcliffe. I'm going to make you a heaping portion of my rice pudding just as soon as I'm able," Mahala promised.

"I'd like that, Miss Simons, but really it's not necessary." He started to walk back to his horse. "I'm just glad that I could help. You take care of yourself." He tipped his hat to bid them goodbye. He gave Mahala a small wink with his soulful eyes. "Take care and don't worry, you will recover in no time. Nice to meet you both!"

CHAPTER 24
Mahala

IT HAD BEEN THREE WEEKS and still Mahala's letter to Ruby had gone unanswered. Mahala was beginning to worry that her request was too great for her dear friend. Of course it was. How could she expect Ruby to support her when she had her own family to worry about? She was still a newlywed and most likely wanted her privacy to start her life with her husband. Surely there would be a child that would be on the way shortly, and Ruby wouldn't have the space for her in their small one-bedroom apartment in New York. Still, something was nagging at her about Ruby's lack of response. It wasn't like Ruby to just ignore her.

On a hunch, Mahala decided to pay Mr. Radcliffe a visit. First, she made a batch of her famous rice pudding she had promised him as his thank you gift. After it thickened, she spooned the treat into two glass jars, wrapped them in tea towels, and secured them with a small strip of twine. Outside, she put the jars in the bicycle's basket.

Mahala mounted her bicycle with a slight hesitation. The bike had been repaired—it looked almost new, remarkably—and her injuries had healed, but the pain of her crash still lingered in her memory. But she set her shoulders and resolved to be brave. Even taking her time to ride at a safe, slow pace, she could make it to Mr. Radcliffe's house and back before dinnertime.

Along the way, Mahala noticed several St. Vincent parrots and instinctively began to count them. She was struck by the memory of the game she used to play with her mother when she was a young girl. A wave of guilt washed over her when she thought about how her decision to leave her family home would hurt Kavita.

She parked her bicycle outside of Mr. Radcliffe's house, grabbed the two jars from her basket, and sauntered down his walkway to announce herself. Mr. Radcliffe himself answered the door.

"Oh, Miss Simons, what a surprise! What are you doing here in Calliaqua?" Mr. Radcliffe exclaimed.

"I wanted to bring you the rice pudding that I promised you," Mahala answered as she placed her gift into his waiting hands.

Mr. Radcliffe gladly accepted it and motioned for her to come into the sitting room. Mahala followed while he deposited the jars on the coffee table. "I appreciate your very thoughtful gift, but it was really unnecessary."

"Oh, that's okay. I love to cook, and it's the least I could do, really. There is something I need to ask you, though." She didn't want to insult him or accuse him of anything. She came here to get answers. "Mr. Radcliffe, are you entirely sure that you posted my letter that day you took me home from the hospital? The reason I'm asking is because it was addressed to my best friend in New York, and she always answers me right away—but it's been three weeks with no response."

"Yes, I'm certain I posted it along with the letters my wife gave me."

Mahala's hopes deflated, but she had to know for certain. "Would you mind just checking your satchel to make sure?"

"Of course," Mr. Radcliffe said obligingly. He limped into the kitchen, squeezing himself to the side of the doorway so his broad-shouldered son could pass through at the same time.

"Oh . . . hi, Mahala. What a nice surprise." Ben's face registered a smile.

"Hi, I hope I'm not interrupting anything. I—I just came to see your father." She reached up to check that her hair was not out of place, suddenly glad she had secured it with a scarf for her bike ride. She hadn't noticed how good-looking he was when she met him the day of her accident. Her cheeks flushed as he walked closer to her.

"All better now?" Ben asked.

"Uh . . . oh . . . yes, fully recovered."

"Don't take this the wrong way, but you looked pretty banged up when I saw you last."

Mahala composed herself and smiled pleasantly at Ben. "It's nice that your father is involved with your work. I can tell he's proud of you."

"Yeah, the leg gives him a little trouble, but otherwise he's strong as an ox. I'm lucky that he's still willing to help me."

Mr. Radcliffe returned with the well-worn satchel in his hand. Face ashen and eyes downcast, he plunked the leather bag down on the coffee table. "I found this stuck to the bottom of my bag." He held up Mahala's small lightweight envelope and bit his lower lip. Mahala felt bad for him but also relieved—Ruby had simply never received the letter.

"I'm so sorry, Miss Simons. It must have gotten separated from my lot, and I was in a rush—I hadn't wanted to leave you waiting for too long. It's totally my fault! How can I make it up to you? Do you want me to post it now?"

Mahala could trust only herself to get it done. "Would you mind taking me in your cart? It will be faster than riding my bicycle and that way I can still make the air mail for today."

"I could take you," Ben cut in.

"If that's okay with Miss Simons . . ." Mr. Radcliffe's eyes flicked from Ben to Mahala.

"Of course, if it's no trouble." she answered.

"Come on, I'll throw your bike in the back, and we can get going right now. I'll even bring you home if you like." Ben motioned to Mahala and politely stepped aside to let her step in front of him to go out the door. "This must be an important letter." He lifted her to the seat of the cart and climbed up next to her.

"You could say that." She kept her scarf in her pocket, allowing her hair to flow freely this time. She noticed Ben looking at her instead of the road ahead of them and smiled. "Tell me what you like best about your business, and don't say the money!" she said playfully. He took a moment before he answered. "Honestly, I love my ladies!" Mahala's eyebrows shot up. How could he think this was a good answer? "You know the ones I mean, right?" he went on. "The old ladies who can barely see, but they press fruit right up to their noses, almost inside their nostrils before they decide to buy. It almost seems like they're going to take a bite too!" He started to laugh. She giggled in relief. "You're too much!" Mahala realized that this was the most at ease she had felt with someone, other than her family, in a long time.

When they arrived back at her house, she allowed Ben to lift her down from the cart. She found that she didn't want their conversation to end. "Thanks so much for your help today. I really enjoyed the company." She held his gaze, smoothing her skirt.

"It was my pleasure. In fact, what would you say to me coming next week to take you on walk, or a picnic?"

Mahala paused for only a second before she answered, "I would like that very much." She smiled, surprising herself at just how much she wanted to see him again.

CHAPTER 25

Mahala

Mahala walked out to join her mother for breakfast and found her staring into her teacup, looking pensive at the kitchen table.

Kavita looked up and her look brightened. "Good morning, my beautiful girl. How are you feeling?"

"I'm fine, Mai. You don't have to worry about me, I promise."

Kavita had helped Mahala following the accident because it was hard for her to raise her arms over her head to dress and undress—and to reach the back of her head. Mahala had always brushed her hair one hundred strokes each night before bed, just as Jane had taught her. This took some time since her voluminous hair reached down to her waist, but Kavita had been patient.

"Sweetling, I'm so glad you are feeling much better now." She took a long pause. "I don't want you to get upset, but I would like you to meet someone." She held up her hand when Mahala opened her mouth in protest. "Hear me out. Jagan Agarwal is a respectable man who runs his father's boat building business on Barbados and travels frequently between Barbados and St. Vincent. He's thirty-five—a perfect age to get married—and Jane confirmed that he is looking for a wife. Henry verified his reputation with friends in Barbados as well." Kavita proffered a photograph of the handsome gentleman for her daughter to inspect. "He would make a wonderful match for you, and you could give him many beautiful children."

Mahala looked at her steely-eyed until her mother set the picture down on the table. Kavita pulled a sheet of paper out of her apron pocket, unfolding it slowly. "Look, if you don't want to meet *him*—Henry gave me a list of men that he thinks are perfectly suitable for you." She walked out of the room without another word.

Mahala felt the walls closing in on her from all sides. She understood why they were coercing her to accept an arranged marriage, but she did not want to bend to their will when she had a will of her own. She thought briefly, jealously, of Henry, who had married for love—twice!—without anyone so much as blinking and had gotten everyone else to alter their needs to accommodate his ambitions—for medical school, for the care of his children—while she couldn't even decide just her own. *The nerve of him*, she thought. *He can't even manage his own life, and he wants to have a hand in mine.*

Just then, there came a knock. Mahala stepped toward the door, but Kavita bustled in and passed her, giving her a meaningful huff of disappointment before she yanked the door open. Ben stood in the doorway, a purple star orchid in hand.

"I thought you might fancy a walk this morning, Miss Simons, if your mother permits," he said. Kavita looked momentarily dumbstruck, raising her eyebrows at her daughter slowly.

"Thank you, yes, that sounds lovely," Mahala said quickly, eager to get out of the house. Ben handed the orchid to Kavita, who took it with a slow smile while Mahala slipped her feet into her shoes.

As she walked with Ben about the garden, Mahala enjoyed his stories of where he planned to be in the future. He told her about making his small market stall into a commercial business with local sourcing of the freshest ingredients and offering delivery not only all over the island but also to others nearby. He wanted to make a name for himself and build his reputation. Mahala admired his enthusiasm. She shared that she too wished to have an accomplishment of her own. She just wasn't sure of what that would be at this point. He was supportive and encouraged her.

As they turned back toward the house, the thought occurred to her that she could possibly keep her parents' interference in her life at bay if she hinted that she was interested in Ben. It was far from a hardship to spend time with him. He wasn't like any of the other men that they tried to match her up with. He was interested in more than finding a wife to have his babies.

CHAPTER 26
Henry

HENRY ROSE EARLY AND SLIPPED out of the house before Carolina and the kids were awake. He had started having breakfast at the hospital instead of his own home in order to avoid its chaos. Carolina was not an organized woman. She was sweet and beautiful and had other good qualities, but running a house efficiently was not in her repertoire. Ever the perfectionist, Henry liked order. Carolina's housekeeping might not be up to his standards, but he had become skilled at getting his way with all of the women in his life—and, as he entered the hospital this morning, it occurred to him that Mahala could be of use to him now.

The more he mulled it over, the more ingenious the idea seemed, if he did say so himself. He would arrange for coverage of his patient's cases with his colleagues and book a trip home to St. Vincent. He knew he would have to have a conversation with her face to face. She would not refuse him.

Days later, Henry arrived on St. Vincent, kissed his mother and daughters, and promptly found Mahala. She welcomed him into the kitchen, preparing them each a cup of chai with a tidiness he missed. He was confident in the logic of his plan. After all the necessary pleasantries were finished, Henry launched into his proposal.

"Look, you've told me many times of your desire to leave this island and make a life for yourself, right? Well, why don't you come back to Panama with me?" Henry said like it was the most natural thing in the world. He wanted to position this so she would see it as a solution to her problem, not as a solution to his.

"What?" She raised her eyebrows. "What are you talking about?"

"I'm talking about you moving into my house in Panama. You could live with me, with my family, far away from this island."

"That doesn't make sense," she said slowly. He could see her sharp mind thinking. "Why would I want to do that? That's not me gaining my independence. That's me trading my present situation to being under your thumb."

"It's a chance for you to be independent from your mother," Henry offered, blowing on his chai.

"Just to be now dependent on you? You must be mad."

"Carolina is overwhelmed with running a house, and I just think that she needs some support and encouragement."

"Isn't that what you're for? I mean, *you* are her husband, right?" Her eyes pierced into her brother's.

"Mahala, you could show her how to be efficient. She could learn from you. Can't you see that this helps us both?"

"This doesn't help us both. This helps *you.* I always knew you were selfish, but this goes beyond that." Her eyes narrowed. "You're trying to manipulate me into thinking that I'm doing something good for myself when I'm only helping to make your life easier. You always had Mama wrapped around your little finger, but I'm not Mama." She held eye contact with him, and he did his best not to squirm.

"Mahala, you're being dramatic. Of course, Mama does what I ask. She wants the best for me. I've been a loving and attentive son, and she sees that."

"I'm not doubting that you love her, I'm just saying that you always find a way to get what you want no matter the cost to the rest of your family. You've got Mama *and me* raising your daughters because it's not convenient for you to mix your two families together. Have you thought about how much that hurts Sofia and Lily?"

He pushed his chair back and walked to the window. "That's really not your concern, Mahala. I've made some sacrifices that were not easy for me, and I'm living with the consequences."

"What consequences are *you* living with?"

Henry stood silent. She rose and took a few steps toward him.

"Your girls are growing up without you. You won't let them come back to Panama because it's not easy for your new wife to accept them? They're your flesh and blood!"

Henry was shocked—she had a lot of nerve. She should be grateful to him for how he looked after her when she was a small girl.

"You have money," she went on. "Why don't you hire a maid?"

"I don't know why you are getting so upset," he sputtered. "I thought we could work something out that would be beneficial for us both. It's obvious that you don't want to help yourself."

He watched her stiffen. "You want me to be where I am of use to you and where you can keep an eye on me at the same time. I'm sorry, Henry, you'll have to figure another way to get what you want this time." She turned on her heel and left him standing alone, wondering what his next move should be.

CHAPTER 27

Mahala

Early Sunday morning, Mahala stood debating two outfit choices to wear to church. Henry had left on yesterday's afternoon ship with only a nod goodbye, but his irritation was worth avoiding the undoubtedly huge mistake of getting sucked into his plans.

"The green one, sweetling," Kavita interrupted, knocking on the door. Mahala looked down at the cotton dress embroidered with white stitching along its delicate lace collar and cuffs. "Such a beautiful silhouette on you. Let me know when you need help with the buttons." Mahala nodded and reached for it. Stubborn as she was about following her family's suggestions, maybe not *everything* needed a show of resistance.

They heard a beautiful sermon at church, chatted with Elizabeth and gave hugs to her children on the church steps, and returned home for the usual refreshments with Jane and John. Kavita insisted on making a quick stop to pick up a few fresh mangos for her fruit plate, insisting the couple go on ahead without them.

Half an hour later, Mahala and Kavita walked into their house to find the living room full of unexpected guests—unexpected only to Mahala, it quickly became clear: a strange, well-dressed man and two other people who could only be the man's parents, who all stopped chatting with Jane and John and looked up at her with a smile when she stepped in.

This was an ambush. Mahala was incensed but contained her fury. Kavita had gone ahead with the meeting without her agreement—and brought in Jane and John as added pressure.

"Hello, Mr. and Mrs. Agarwal. It's lovely of you to come to our home. And this must be your son," Kavita cooed with a nod of acknowledgment.

"Yes, hello, Mrs. Patandine. It's lovely to meet you and your daughter. This is Jagan. He's home on a visit from Barbados." Mr. Agarwal stood and put a hand on his son's shoulder. "We're so lucky to have him so close. If the boat ride wasn't so short and convenient, I'm not sure we would see him so often," he joked with a warm smile. "It's important for families to stay close. Don't you agree?"

"Oh, yes, of course. Family is everything. Mahala is my only daughter, so naturally I want her close by when the time comes for her to marry and start a family," Kavita answered.

Mahala smiled tightly to avoid screaming. A man of thirty-five shouldn't have to rely on his parents for more than an introduction.

"May I offer you some fresh mango?" her mother continued.

"Yes, that's very kind of you," Mrs. Agarwal chirped. She made eye contact with her son, prodding him to enter the conversation.

"Oh, I love mango this time of year. Not many people know that it is the number one consumed fruit in the world!" he almost shouted. Small beads of perspiration appeared at the sides of his temples.

Mahala had to force herself not to roll her eyes. This process seemed so awkward and pointless. It was painful to watch him attempt to position himself as a suitable match in front of his parents. She calculated just how pleasant she had to be not to embarrass her parents while still stopping short of encouraging him. Even she did not want a repeat of the disastrous event that happened when they tried to marry her off when she was just thirteen.

"I'll help you prepare the mango, Mai," Mahala sang out, attempting to follow Kavita into the kitchen.

"Oh no, sweetling, you stay here and entertain our guests. I'll be out momentarily." Kavita glided into the kitchen and shortly called out to Jane for help.

The awkwardness did not ease in the living room. After a long silence, Kavita returned with the mango, its deep golden yellow flesh glistening against the stark white serving platter, while Jane carried a tray with a cold bottle of white wine and seven glasses.

"So, Jagan, tell us a little about your business. Your father says you are indispensable," John began. Mahala was grateful that John was trying to kindle the sluggish conversation.

"That's welcome praise from my father, but I must admit that things are going well. Dad's boat business mostly concentrated on repairs of fishing and leisure crafts, but I've been able to move the business more toward customizing and designing boat interiors. The possibilities are limitless," Jagan gushed. "In my business I spent quite a bit of time going back and forth from St. Vincent to Barbados. Presently I live in Barbados but . . . if I had reason to return to St. Vincent, I might consider that." Jagan looked at Mahala intently.

"Mahala, maybe you would like to see the Agarwals' business operations," John suggested.

"Oh yes, that sounds interesting," Mahala replied dutifully, her hands folded in her lap. She had no intention of ever setting foot in his place of business.

Another silence settled over them. Jane smoothed her skirt repeatedly and adjusted her position in her seat. John tapped his index finger in an increasingly faster pattern as he looked at Mahala and Jagan.

"Would anyone care for a glass of white wine?" Kavita interjected. She immediately reached for the tray and started to fill the glasses one by one. To Mahala's delight, that drew the focus away from the stilted conversation.

"My mother tells me that you enjoy sewing. Did you make that dress that you are wearing?" Jagan tapped his foot as he spoke.

"Yes, I make most of my dresses," Mahala declared. When he smiled but said nothing, she reluctantly added, "But I enjoy more things than sewing. I also tutor young students, including my nieces, in reading and writing."

"Oh, that sounds interesting for a young lady such as yourself."

"You could say that." Mahala glanced at her watch. Kavita shot her a glare.

"I didn't mean to offend you, Miss Simons. I'm genuinely interested in getting to know you," Jagan explained.

She sighed. "You didn't offend me. I just have a bit of a headache."

"Oh, I'm so sorry to hear that." Jagan glanced over at his parents and stood. "We'll let you get some rest. It was lovely to meet you Miss Simons, Mr. and Mrs. Simons, Mrs. Patandine. Thank you for the refreshments. I look forward to calling on you again in the future." Jagan guided his parents out the door as he gave a final wave to Mahala's family.

Mahala wasted no time in getting out of the house as soon as the Agarwal family left. She wanted to relay this latest ploy to Ben. He didn't make his usual visit to her house today, so she quickly hopped on her bike and arrived at the Radcliffe house in no time. She knocked hard on the door and was relieved when Ben answered. "I was just feeling bad that I didn't make it over to your house today, and then you show up here!" He waved her in the house. "What's going on?"

"I just needed to see a friendly face. They ambushed me," Mahala explained.

"Who did they line up this time? A prince?"

"More like a frog," she teased him back.

"Better a frog than a dragon. I would have to slay him for you, and I wouldn't want blood on my royal hands," he teased. Mahala couldn't hold back her laughter at his silliness. He managed to lift her mood once again.

CHAPTER 28

Mahala

One week later, Mahala heard Kavita come in with the post. As soon as her mother had cleared the parlor, she rushed to the table by the front door and leafed through the letters quickly. There in the middle of the stack was one envelope with the signature blue and red striped border indicating air mail. It was postmarked from New York. There was also a parcel addressed to her. She plucked the letter out of the stack, scooped up the small package, and retreated to her room, where she gently slid her letter opener under the envelope's corner flap.

Ruby Govia
245 E. 116th Street
New York City, New York 10029
Dear Mahala,

I was glad to receive your letter. Jerome and I were beginning to worry about you since we hadn't heard from you in quite some time. I'm so sorry that you've had to endure all of that pressure from Henry and your parents. I think you're being too hard on yourself though. It's not your fault that Violet died.

Of course we would be glad to host you in our house. I would never dream of denying my dearest friend my help.

I have spoken to my supervisor, and he is willing to give you a position as a seamstress as soon as you arrive in New York. The pay starts by piecework but if you are fast and efficient you can make a decent wage. As you might expect, there are some politics to contend with in the shop. The bold ladies get better projects so if you watch like a hawk when the orders come in, you can swoop in and get the higher paying garments. I have a feeling you won't have any trouble handling this. We are supposed to be a union shop, but the owner is very sly and knows how to get around this. We are constantly fighting to get better conditions in the shop, but it is hard to keep the pressure on. Many women realize it would be better if we walked out, but they have families to feed and can't risk losing wages in the near term for the promise of higher wages if we fight.

You will have to sleep on the sofa in the living room, but I will do my best to make it comfortable for you. Jerome and I tend to retire early in the evening so you will be able to have some privacy.

As soon as you have arranged for your travel from St. Vincent to New York, let me know the details so I can arrange to pick you up. Jerome and I will meet you at the port when your ship comes in. When you are interviewed for the ship's manifest, you should list me as your sister so they don't question where you will stay and how you will support yourself. You will have alien status in the United States, which permits you to stay only on a temporary basis, so don't give anything away regarding your intention to stay.

I am so looking forward to our reunion.

Love always,
Ruby

Mahala was relieved that Ruby was so eager to welcome her into her home. She then turned her attention to slicing open the parcel. Inside she found a small item nested and wrapped in several layers of crumpled newspaper. She peeled open the little packet to reveal a familiar treasure: the prized tiger cowrie shell she had given to Ruby when she'd left the island for New York. Mahala's mouth dropped open, her hand flying to her heart, instantly warmed by Ruby's sentimental gesture.

She had to begin planning how she would deliver the news to her mother—and Jane and John as well. They were all bound to be angry. She hoped that they would eventually understand her decision, even if they didn't agree.

But she couldn't wait to tell Ben the good news. He at least would be glad for her.

As had become their habit, he knocked on her door in the late morning after church the next day. She threw open the door and smiled from ear to ear.

"Ben, you won't believe it." She pulled him inside and swung the door closed. "Come on, let's go out to the garden. I have some really big news."

He grinned. "It's nice to see you so happy. What's going on?" She rushed him through the house and out the back to a secluded corner, grasping his hands excitedly.

"I'm finally getting my chance to do something for my life. I'm really doing it." Her eyes opened wide.

He shook his head, smiling. "What are you talking about?"

"I'm moving to New York! Ruby agreed to let me stay with her! I'm getting a real job!" The words spilled out of her like a waterfall.

Ben stood still. His mouth gaped open. "I—I don't understand. You're leaving, just like that?"

"I want my life to mean something. I want to do something. I told you that I was trying to figure it out. You agreed with me. You told me I'd find it soon—and I have."

"I . . . I . . . what about us?"

"What about us?" Her brows knit together.

"I'm in love with you, Mahala. I thought you felt the same way." He gently cradled her face in his hands and kissed her.

Mahala pulled back, startled. Hurt danced across Ben's face. "You know how strongly I feel about my independence. Don't you see that this is my chance? To see more of the world? I need to do this."

"I know. Just stay . . . for me . . . with me . . ." He trailed off. "You can do what you want. I won't stand in your way. Figure out what you want here."

He really loved her. Mahala felt torn, confused. Being with him was a refuge from her usual life. It was easy and fun, and they agreed on most things. They had talked about the future, but she hadn't realized it was their *shared* future. She wanted the life she imagined for herself as an independent woman with a job and a purpose of her own . . . but she did eventually want to get married and have a family. Ben was a kind, interesting, sweet man and she could see herself falling in love with him—who else would promise her such freedom in a marriage? She knew she would risk losing him if she left, and yet . . .

"I really care for you, Ben, but—but I have to do what is right for me. I'm sorry." She felt tears sting her eyes unexpectedly.

"Can I hope that you'll change your mind?" he asked wistfully.

"You can, but I don't think I will." She kissed him on the cheek, and they said their goodbyes.

CHAPTER 29

Mahala

MAHALA TOOK A DEEP BREATH, trying to shake the grief of her conversation with Ben from her mind. With one hard conversation down, she might as well commit to a terrible day and get the worst one behind her. She strode into the kitchen looking for her mother, but the house was empty. *Just as well*, she thought, squaring her shoulders, and marched over to Jane and John's house where she found all three of them huddled around steaming cups of tea. She must have looked like she had an announcement to make because they all went quiet and looked up at her.

"I'm glad I found the three of you here. I'll have to say this only once," Mahala began, gently but firmly. She thought about how to soften the news, but the truth burst out. "I'm leaving St. Vincent. This is not a decision that I have come to easily. I don't want to fight." Kavita inhaled sharply and set her cup down.

Mahala tucked a stray lock of her ebony hair behind her ear and turned to face John. "When Dai was killed, I understood your need to assume a fatherly role in my life. You naturally felt an obligation to ensure his wish that I be married would happen. An unmarried woman is—is a burden, I know." She swallowed hard and took a deep breath. "Believe it or not, my leaving isn't really because you all want to arrange my marriage—it's just that I want to see what else there is out there for me.

"Ruby has assured me that there is a place for me in New York City, living with her and her husband. She has arranged a job for me where she works in the Garment District as a seamstress starting as soon as I can get myself there. I am hoping to have your blessing, but I am intent on going anyway." Mahala paused briefly to allow her parents to process what she had said. Her large brown eyes pleaded for understanding but were set for resistance from the collective.

"Mahala, this is not how I raised you to behave!" Kavita cried. "What about your duty to this family and our reputation?"

"It's quite scandalous for you to go to New York as an unmarried woman," Jane snapped.

"How will I explain to our neighbors and friends that you just up and left your obligations to your family and will live on your own?" Kavita's voice started to shake. "I—I don't understand how you can do this to me. Have you no shame?" She threw her hands into the air.

"Mai, I just want to have something of my own. I want to choose the man I am going to marry for myself." She crouched down beside her mother and embraced her comfortingly. Kavita accepted the gesture and lifted her hand up to her face to catch her own tears.

"What about Ben? Does he want you to go?" she asked pointedly.

"This is not about Ben. Going to New York will give me a chance to become an independent woman. I will decide my own destiny. Maybe that's not the destiny you envisioned for me, but it's the one I envision for myself. My whole life I've done what was expected of me—I learned to run the household, I helped with Lily and Sofia, I set aside my studies."

"You spent far too much time with Henry's books than you should have. I never should have allowed it," said Jane.

Mahala felt a surge of frustration. She rose from Kavita and threw herself into the open kitchen chair. "I *still* feel jealous of Henry's education and the opportunity that he had to go to medical school to become a doctor. I would've liked to continue my education. It's too late for that now, but I'm a grown woman and I can make this decision for myself. I'm sorry if this makes you unhappy, but my mind is made up. And don't involve Ben in this. He knows why I'm going to New York."

"I'm not going to give you any financial support if you leave this house," Kavita threatened. Mahala watched Jane and John exchange a look. "They won't give you any money either," her mother spat.

"I know I'll have to support myself if I leave home. I've saved some money, and there's a job waiting for me," Mahala explained. Her eyes moved to each of her three parents. She searched for understanding but came up empty.

"Sweetling," Kavita pleaded, her tone shifting, "a young woman should be married at your age, not trying to make it on her own in the world. Don't be foolish. Look at what Ruby has. Yes, she moved to New York but she's a married woman. You have so much to offer the right man. Let us find the right match for you."

Mahala thought briefly, painfully, of Ben and the way he'd kissed her so tenderly, the way he could have been the compromise her mother would've been all too delighted to find. But she didn't *want* to compromise.

"Mai, you care too much about what the community will think if I disobey your wishes," Mahala said accusingly. "That's what's really important to you."

"You're right—I care about our reputations, yours and mine. If you leave like this, you'll bring shame on all of us," Kavita said. Her dark eyes glistened with fresh tears. "Don't do this."

"Mai, the fact that you're withdrawing financial support proves to me that I *need* to go my own way and support myself. I won't let financial threats sway my decision. I love you, and Mama and Papa too, but I need to do this." She took a deep breath in to bolster her resolve. "I hope one day you'll understand and forgive me." Tears stung her eyes.

Kavita hung her head in her hands, almost reaching her lap. "I don't think you're going to get what you're searching for by going to New York. The world is a harsh place to be on your own," she warned.

"We won't support this either." John pounded his fist on the table and rose from his chair. "You are making a huge mistake, Mahala."

"I'm sorry you feel that way." Mahala whisked herself out of her chair and left as quickly as possible. As the door swung closed behind her, she heard Kavita wail.

CHAPTER 30
Mahala

October 1921

MAHALA SORTED THROUGH HER THINGS, deliberately setting aside items that would be of no use to her in New York in October. She would have to make some adjustments to the style of her current wardrobe to live in the most fashionable city in the world. Ruby had told her to pack carefully and lightly because space was at a premium at her small apartment. She would need to either borrow a few heavier weight items from Ruby or buy warmer clothing when she arrived. She was leaving the warm eighty-eight-degree weather in St. Vincent for a chilly sixty degrees in New York. The winter would literally be freezing or worse. However, Ruby spoke of how beautiful the fall in New York could be. Mahala longed to see the trees that changed color to bright orange, red, and gold before they dropped their leaves for the winter.

She had read an article about a magnificent place called Central Park that was designed by architects Frederick Law Olmsted and Calvert Vaux in the 1850s and stretched a full two and half miles from top to bottom in the middle of Manhattan. She was curious to see its large lake, rolling lawns, and woodland areas bordered by winding paths. The article explained the park was built for people to escape the hard concrete and brick structures of the city and enjoy a taste of nature. Central Park would be at the top of her list of sites to see in New York City. According to Ruby, her and Jerome's apartment was just a fifteen to twenty-minute walk away from the top entrance to the park.

Mahala tried to put aside the deep emotional conflict she felt as she packed. She would miss her family and watching her two young nieces grow up. Henry was lucky that Jane had agreed to take over their rearing. Despite the harsh words of their argument, Jane was a good mother and a wonderful grandmother. Mahala was also glad to be getting farther away from Henry as well. It was obvious that he was trying to find a use for her to benefit himself. If she stashed herself away in New York it wouldn't be easy for him to influence her.

She felt sad that she was leaving Ben behind, especially after his revelation. He was a good man, and she had depended on his friendship and support. She hoped that she was not making a mistake by choosing what she wanted for herself instead of giving them a chance at a life together.

Mahala's thoughts returned to the task at hand. She managed to squeeze her belongings into one large trunk and a small valise. She locked the trunk and affixed the handwritten label to the top, stating her name and address with perfect penmanship. However, her cursive letters still slanted to the left even after she had been forced to write with her right hand long ago. She pushed her trunk to the front of the house and walked back to retrieve her valise. She pinched open the kiss lock to her floral needlepoint purse, eased open the metal frame, and slipped her passport into the cream-colored silk moiré lining, along with her traveling gloves, one lipstick, and twenty-five US dollars she had exchanged for her British pounds. The cash was all she had to her name and would have to last her until she started working in New York. With careful planning she would manage. She had prepaid her passage for both the ferry over to Barbados, where she would stay with her aunt for a night, and then the larger sailing ship for her voyage to New York.

The morning of her departure, Mahala dreaded saying goodbye to her parents. She had already had her tearful farewell with Henry's girls and with Elizabeth and her children. She had reassured her sister that she would be fine on her own. Still, Elizabeth made her promise to ask her for help if she had problems in New York.

Mahala had asked her parents to come to breakfast before seeing her off. Kavita had helped ready the food in uncharacteristic silence and was looking sadly into her chai when they heard the door open. As Jane and John came in, their faces drooped, looking as if they were attending a wake instead of saying bon voyage.

Mahala gently kissed them both, and they all sat down to the food Kavita had prepared. "It's not like I'm never going to see you again. I promise, I'll be back." Mahala served a helping of fresh fruit to each of them.

Kavita sniffed, dabbing a tear from the corner of her eye. "I know, but it feels so final. And—and I know you think you can take on the world, but you're putting yourself in danger without the protection of a man."

Mahala sliced the omelet in quarters, taking a slow deliberate breath before she responded to her mother's same tired concerns. "Mai, I'll be fine." She dropped the egg onto her plate and quickly shoved a forkful into her mouth. Kavita looked at Jane and then John. They both maintained their frosty exterior, pushing food around their plates without really eating a bite.

Just then, a knock pierced the silence. Mahala jumped up to answer and was relieved to see Ben. He had arrived early to bring her to the ferry. She pulled him in the door. "Perfect timing. Come, can you help me with my things?" She whisked him past the kitchen and called back, "Ben's here. We're just going to get my luggage loaded."

John sat glued to his seat. Ordinarily he would be the first to offer to help. As she and Ben loaded the wagon, she told herself that she didn't have much longer to endure their anger and disappointment. She would soon be on her way to her great adventure. Mahala gathered her resolve, hugged Kavita, Jane, and John, and reminded them of how much she loved them. She then dashed out the door with Ben to make the ferry.

The ride to the ferry landing was quiet, Ben sinking into silence between her attempts at small talk. Imagining what Ben had to be risking emotionally to help her, she felt a pang of guilt. They arrived with just enough time for a porter to whisk her bags onto the ship, leaving them standing together awkwardly, wistfully.

"I don't know what I would've done without your friendship and support," Mahala said. She kissed him lightly on his cheek. He pulled her in for a hug and kissed her back. She held his stare, feeling his heart pounding. "You know where to find me." He choked out a laugh and gave her a wink. She nodded, smiling at him, then walked away with a deep breath to board the ferry. Before she disappeared into the doorway of the boat, she turned, giving him a final wave.

The SS *Vauban* was an impressive steam ship. It was a beautifully appointed passenger vessel, the largest and most luxurious ocean liner with service between Buenos Aires and New York. Mahala was fortunate to be able to pay for passage by herself since she was now on her own financially. However, she still had to share a cabin in order to be able to afford it. She had been lucky to get a wonderful cabin mate the last time she traveled to Panama—indeed, she wondered what Cynthia was up to and wished her only good things—so she was hoping for the same for this long voyage.

She found her cabin number printed on her ticket and flagged down a porter in a starched white jacket with gleaming brass buttons. He escorted her to her cabin and helped her with her luggage. He gracefully swung the door open for her to enter and motioned her inside. There she found her cabin mate already stowing her belongings. She was a tall, slim woman with a medium complexion and an angular face. She was dressed well in a cotton dress with nary a wrinkle and freshly shined patent leather shoes. Mahala appreciated the detail of her outfit right down to her shoes' single strap, center buckle, and a matching handbag.

She introduced herself as Mrs. Lambert and displayed a pleasant smile and shining eyes. Mahala liked the air of sophistication the older woman gave off. She settled in to unpack some of her belongings.

Mrs. Lambert proved to be a charming woman who was interested in everything Mahala had to say. She paid rapt attention to her every word, often placing her gloved hand on top of Mahala's to convey her understanding of Mahala's decision to break from her family and start an independent life. Mahala thought it was slightly strange that after their many conversations she still knew very little about Mrs. Lambert, yet she had divulged so much about her own life to the woman.

They spent most of their time together enjoying the beautiful hotel-like atmosphere of the luxury ocean liner. The vessel to Panama had been beautiful, but Mahala had never seen as much opulence in her life as she did on this ship. The sitting salon could rival any solarium. It had high ceilings and large windows positioned along the top perimeter of the room. The windows were surrounded by glossy carved moldings painted a gleaming white. Large potted plants stood in each corner of the room, anchoring the seating area holding several large, round mahogany tables and leather chairs. The walls were deep walnut with fluted paneling running vertically across the entire length of the room. Each table had a brass tray with pre-made cocktail refreshments for the passengers to enjoy at their leisure.

Mahala enjoyed the nightly entertainment in the grand ballroom, which featured a piano player and singer. Many passengers took to the dance floor and looked elegant in their black-tie formal dress. Mahala knew how to dance, but she preferred her conversations with Mrs. Lambert and their dinner table companions. They all sampled a new cocktail made with lime juice and gin called a gimlet. They were told by the steward that British Royal Naval officers often drank this concoction when they were at sea to stave off scurvy due to the high levels of vitamin C in the lime juice.

Mrs. Lambert enjoyed the gimlet so much that she ordered another round for everyone. The second one seemed to go to her head because she stumbled when she got up from the table to excuse herself. Mahala leaped out of her seat to come to her cabin mate's aid. She reached her left arm under Mrs. Lambert's right to steady her and made her apologies to their companions, bidding them a goodnight. Mahala guided her down the ship's hallways as Mrs. Lambert's momentum swayed the two of them from one side to the other, banging the side of the hall several times. Mahala was fighting to keep making forward progress without falling down. Her shoulder would surely be bruised from the last bump she took to her right side. The cocktails tasted like mostly lime juice to Mahala, so she wasn't sure how Mrs. Lambert got so drunk so fast.

When they reached their cabin Mahala propped her charge against the wall just to the left of the door and reached across her body for the key in her purse.

That's when she noticed that the kiss lock to her purse was not securely closed. It must have opened when they knocked into the wall on their turbulent walk down the ship's hallway. She got Mrs. Lambert inside and spilled her onto her bed, removed her shoes, and put her purse and gloves on her nightstand. She didn't bother trying to get her into her nightgown. Mrs. Lambert needed a good night's rest and would be right as rain in the morning, of that Mahala was sure.

CHAPTER 31
Mahala

New York City

On the last day of the voyage, they each packed and closed their trunks and rang for the porter. Mahala was excited to finally arrive in New York to be reunited with her best friend. As they approached the harbor, she squinted at the crowd but couldn't spot her.

The passengers filed down the gangway of the massive ship that stood four decks tall. Mahala emerged about a quarter of the way through the procession.

"Mahala! Over here!" She heard a voice and spun around, looking wildly through the crowd, holding her pea green cloche hat to her head with a gloved hand for fear someone would bump it off. She spotted Ruby waving her arms frantically to get her attention. Ruby nearly knocked into the waiting woman next to her, rushed ahead of Jerome, and ran to meet Mahala when she stepped clear of the gangway.

"Oh, it's so good to see you!" She wrapped her arms around Mahala and squeezed her tightly. "How was the trip? Did you have any trouble? What did you eat? Are you hungry?" Ruby fired questions so fast Mahala didn't have a chance to answer.

"Slow down. It's good to see you, too! Yes, everything was fine on the trip." Jerome caught up and he kissed her cheek in greeting. "I met some nice people and the food was delicious. Our last meal was breakfast this morning, though, so I could do with some lunch if you and Jerome haven't already eaten." Mahala searched for her luggage claim ticket, and Jerome plucked it out of her hands, ever the gentleman. He started off in search of the porter.

"I want to hear all about your journey. Was the SS *Vauban* as luxurious as I read about? Did it really have a two-sided stairway and crystal chandeliers? Did it have fireplaces? Give me some details!"

"It was everything you read and more. The carpets felt like stepping on velvet." Mahala and Ruby followed Jerome as he located Mahala's trunk and, with the porter's help, loaded it into a taxicab. Forty-five minutes later they were in front of the Govias' apartment building. After her trunk was unloaded and she had a chance to freshen up, Mahala was ready to see some of the city.

"Let's go to that little sandwich shop that we passed along the way. You are both so gracious to let me stay with you—let me buy us lunch," Mahala said.

It was unseasonably warm for October at seventy degrees, so contrary to what she had expected for fall in New York, she didn't need a coat. She grabbed her purse, hat, and gloves and whisked out the door with Ruby and Jerome. The happy trio trotted down the sidewalk, sliding into the steady flow of pedestrians on the move. Mahala admired the enormity of the tall buildings—hardly the skyscrapers they'd passed on the drive, yet so much taller than St. Vincent's—and marveled at how so much could fit into one city block. Ruby and Jerome glided over to the right when they saw they were close to the sandwich shop. Unfortunately, Mahala did not pick up on this cue and was nearly run over when she stopped abruptly to follow her friends. She would have to get used to how the crowds moved in her new city.

They ordered a modest lunch; Mahala suspected they were being kind to prevent her having to pay a large bill. When the waiter came with the check, she scooped up the paper—yet when she opened her purse for her wallet, she discovered that it was missing. She searched her entire purse several times and still came up empty.

"I've been robbed!" Mahala was instantly filled with dread and despair. She didn't have a dollar to her name. She couldn't imagine what she was going to do without the money she had so carefully planned to bring to her new home. It was all she had in the world—and there was no way of getting any help from her family.

"Are you sure, Mahala? Let me check for you. Did you put your purse down anywhere?" Ruby asked.

"No, I never let it out of my sight." As the words left her mouth, Mahala recalled the walk back to the cabin with Mrs. Lambert. It occurred to her that Mrs. Lambert might not have been really intoxicated that night, but rather that she was a clever actress and a thief.

"It must have been my cabin mate. I had to take her back to the cabin one night when she got too intoxicated to walk by herself. She was pushing and crashing into me along the way. It must have been during one of those bumps that she was able to get into my purse and steal my money." Mahala's cheeks flushed. How could she be so stupid and trusting of this total stranger?

Jerome remedied the immediate situation by taking care of the bill.

"Do you think you should report the crime to the authorities? I mean the SS *Vauban*, not the New York City police," Ruby asked.

"I don't even know how I'd do such a thing, honestly—or how they'd find her wherever she is now. What if Lambert wasn't even her name? I'll write to the steamship line, I suppose. But I can't imagine anything will come of it."

Mahala was angry that she let herself be taken advantage of, but she was more determined than ever to prove that she could take care of herself.

CHAPTER 32

Mahala

Boris Koifman was an extremely tough Russian Jewish immigrant who had started from nothing when he came to New York. He was now the proud owner of a successful and very profitable garment factory. He was well known to the buyers at Bloomingdale's, Bergdorf Goodman, and Abraham & Straus. He could be nasty and demanding, but he boasted that his workers turned out the highest quality garments in the district. He consistently had the largest orders from all the major department stores in town.

He was largely unfazed by the pressure the International Ladies' Garment Workers' Union put on his business, and threatened to fire any woman who complained about his working conditions. He'd only begrudgingly made the required safety changes in his own factory after the infamous Triangle Shirtwaist Factory fire in 1911. Over one hundred and forty women died in that fire, either trapped inside the building or jumping to their deaths out of windows to escape the flames. Ruby had described it with a shudder. The factory doors had been locked at all times to prevent the workers from either stealing or taking too many breaks.

Mr. Koifman worried about theft as well, she said, but he now employed security guards and did random searches of the workers when they left for the day. "Watch out—they'll rough you up if they think you're walking out with something." That got results, in his opinion.

The smart women like Ruby stayed on Mr. Koifman's good side most of the time. She did what she was told, worked tirelessly, and never complained. Despite her easygoing nature and natural compliance, she had been screamed at numerous times for minor mistakes. "Just be sure to apologize and make things right—even if it wasn't your fault," Ruby sighed. He would often demand that she remake a dress if the hem was an eighth of an inch off from what was specified. Ruby did it without complaint, but she didn't get credit for the completion of that garment until it passed inspection, even if her piece rate went down and her paycheck suffered as a result.

"Honestly, just keep your temper under control when dealing with him, and you'll be all right," Ruby said, trying to sound upbeat. Mahala said a prayer that night for patience. Keeping her temper had never been her strongest suit—and she really needed this job.

"Hurry up, Mahala!" Ruby called through the door. Mahala straightened her short-sleeved white blouse and black skirt, ready for her interview with Mr. Koifman. The short sleeves, although not strictly for the season, would show that she was mindful of the hazards of the sewing machines as well as aware of the warm temperatures of the work environment. She didn't want to embarrass herself or Ruby by not looking prepared. She knew her way around a sewing machine, but this large-scale level of production was totally unfamiliar to her.

Mahala and Ruby rode the subway and emerged on the street for the short walk to Koifman's. As they neared the entrance to the building, the double doors burst open and a push boy ran through wheeling two garment racks, one in each arm. Mahala whipped her head around and jumped out of the way. The racks held twelve dozen dresses tightly packed on hangers. He was headed for a waiting truck, which would take the dresses to their final destination uptown. The invoice for the department store was rolled up and protruding out of his right back pocket. When he came to a stop at the truck, he balanced one rack with his right foot, held the other with his left hand, and reached around his back with his free hand to retrieve the invoice. He wheeled the garments onto the lift gate and into the truck, disappearing from view. Mahala's eyes widened at his speed and finesse.

They entered through the main door of the factory and marched past the secretary directly to the workroom floor. There they found a large two-story room with hardwood floors and ten-foot-tall windows spaced every three feet on all four walls. Although the windows let in a flood of light, as they were designed to do, task lights also hung from the ceiling, shining down on the seamstresses and tailors for when they would be working far into the dark evening hours. Four rows of wooden tables spanned the length of the room, and each row held twelve sewing machines on either side of the table, setting the women across from each other in eight neat rows. Several empty metal garment racks were stored at the back of the room. The women were beginning to get organized for the start of the day by loading their heavy spools of thread into place next to their sewing machines.

A man stood to the side with a cart laden with fabric; Mahala could see that it had been cut into dress patterns already. He began rolling his cart up the aisles to distribute the precut forms to the seamstresses. It was eight thirty in the morning, and already the air felt warm from all the people rushing about.

Ruby spotted her boss in the back of the room talking with one of the young seamstresses. She placed her hand on Mahala's shoulder and looked into her eyes. Raising an eyebrow, she jerked her head to the left to indicate that this was the opportune time to make the introduction. Mahala nodded and followed.

"Mr. Koifman, this is my friend Mahala. You remember that I told you about her needing a job. She's an excellent seamstress." Ruby stepped to the side to allow Mahala to come closer.

"I'll be the judge of that, Ruby." He turned his head and made eye contact with Mahala. "Just arrived in New York, did you?"

"Yes, sir, Mr. Koifman. I arrived yesterday."

"You don't need to call me sir. Mr. Koifman is fine. How much experience do you have in garment making?" Mr. Koifman continued to leaf through his paperwork for today's orders.

"I've made dresses and skirts and done hemming on all kinds of trousers." The truth was that, although Mahala had experience sewing a wide variety of garments, she had only private clients and did not have any professional experience. She had helped to mend the sugar plantation workers' uniforms, but she didn't want to mention it for fear that Mr. Koifman might look down on that. This was a high-quality shop which produced name brand garments. New York was fast becoming an important hub in the fashion industry, even if mostly what was produced was imitations of Parisian couture. But Ruby was vouching for her. Mahala hoped that that counted for something.

Mr. Koifman looked up from his paperwork and took in the sight of Mahala. She schooled her face into something pleasant, neutral, determined, but found he was looking at her hands, as if assessing her fingers.

"Well, Ruby's a good judge of character," he said gruffly. "No time like the present! Can you start today?" Mr. Koifman directed his attention to his next task, waving at his secretary to fetch him another cup of coffee.

"Yes!" Mahala chirped with glee. At least she had secured gainful employment. Step one accomplished. Step two was to find a place to live on her own, but that would have to wait until she could save some money.

Ruby took Mahala to the coat room, where they could store their personal belongings under lock and key during the work day. Once she had her coat, hat, gloves, and purse safely secured, Mahala was eager to get to work.

"Come, bubbeleh, sit over here between Ruby and me. I'm Mrs. Leibowitz," a large woman said, ushering Mahala over to her seat. She gave Mahala a welcome nod and then concentrated on her own work. She was ten years older than Ruby and Mahala—but Mahala quickly noticed she was fast as a whip in turning out finished garments. She had the scars on her fingers to prove it.

"I've been jabbed by a needle more times than I can count," she said, when she caught Mahala looking. Ruby barely glanced up from her work. "A hazard of the trade. Just don't get any blood on the garments. I did that once and Mr. Koifman deducted it from my pay."

CHAPTER 33
Mahala

SOON AFTER MAHALA STARTED AT Koifman's, she joined the International Ladies' Garment Workers' Union. It was no secret that Mr. Koifman detested the organization. Although he could not legally prevent them from meeting with their union leaders, he did discourage the ladies from actively participating. She noticed he made sure he had trays brimming with cheese blintzes from Katz's Delicatessen delivered on union meeting days. He knew the ladies couldn't resist the delicate thin pancakes stuffed with sweet cheese and topped with sour cream and fruit sauce—and would schedule the delivery for ten minutes after the union meeting started. Mahala once overheard him instruct his secretary to open the trays to allow the delightful aroma to waft into the meeting room. He didn't have to say anything. He let the blintzes announce themselves. The silent pull of the confection did its job for the most part and kept the meetings brief. He intentionally wasn't playing fair.

Mahala saw through Mr. Koifman's attempt to minimize the union's influence. He continually made disparaging comments about workers who took cigarette breaks to deter them from returning to their stations while wafting the scent of smoke near the fabric, saying, "I don't know how any true lady could stand the smell of such a disgusting and distasteful habit." Embarrassed, the smokers would return to their workstations earlier or skip the breaks altogether.

Mr. Koifman pressured the women to skip lunch breaks or work extremely long hours without additional compensation, stating that *this* overtime was not part of the negotiated settlement, and they were under obligation to finish what he had orders for. If he didn't get paid, he reasoned, he couldn't pay them. And when the girl three seats down was out with pneumonia for two weeks—giving Mahala awful dreams of Violet, fading in the hospital—Mr. Koifman replaced her without notice.

While the other women bowed to his demands, Mahala did not. It was not enough for her to reject this treatment; she knew that she had to convince the other women to stand up for themselves as a group.

She remembered one of her first union meetings, when most of the women were anxious to get back to work as they watched the clock tick by and felt the pressure of falling behind in their orders. Mahala, however, stayed for the entire meeting and made sure she spoke directly to the local leader one on one. The rhetoric she espoused resonated with Mahala. The ILGWU allowed everyone in the industry to join, regardless of job type or skill set. This promoted more unity and solidarity among members, unlike the older-style craft unions that were specific to job function. This meant they had numbers, and numbers were powerful when negotiating with management. Mahala used her natural charm to forge a close working relationship with the local union leader and was able to build a small coalition among Koifman's seamstresses, including Ruby and Mrs. Leibowitz, who monitored and reported back to leadership what was going on in their shop. With the backing of the ILGWU, Mahala was not afraid of using her voice and confronting Mr. Koifman in order to get what the union had already fought for them to have. Unfortunately, she found out that this required a continuous effort.

This morning, Mahala neatly stacked her pile of dresses to be completed next to her sewing machine. Each seamstress had a dedicated section of the worktable for her individual work. After inspection, the garments were moved along to be pressed; then the shop boys would insert hangers and place them on the racks to be inventoried and readied for delivery. When everyone did their part, the operation hummed along steadily like a well-oiled machine.

Mahala and Ruby began to organize their work for the day as the other ladies began to filter into their own workstations. Mrs. Leibowitz was among the first to claim her seat next to the duo.

Mahala admired Mrs. Leibowitz for her work ethic as well as her personal style. Most of the women who worked at Koifman's wore utilitarian clothing, but not Mrs. Leibowitz. She arrived each day in a smart, stylish skirt suit expertly tailored by her own hands, removing her jacket to reveal a crisp, pressed cotton blouse. She always hung her jacket on the back of her chair and got straight to work.

This morning Mahala noticed that when Mrs. Leibowitz arrived, she looked uncharacteristically rumpled. Her hair was loosely pulled back with several tendrils unsecured. She had dark circles under her tired eyes.

"Mrs. Leibowitz, is everything all right?" Mahala asked.

"It was a long night last night." She reached a hand up to smooth her stray locks back into place. "My youngest son kept me up all night. He was burning up and had a terrible cough. I had to take him all the way over to my mother's first thing this morning. I didn't think I was going to make it here on time."

"Oh, I'm so sorry."

"It'll be all right, bubbeleh, he's in good hands with his grandmother." She tucked herself into her work and her machine started to hum.

Mahala started in on her own pile of garments and expertly sewed each of her precut fabric patterns with utmost efficiency. With the amount of work they had to accomplish, the day flew by.

At just about four o'clock, Mr. Koifman burst out of his office onto the shop floor. "Ladies! Attention please! I just received an addition to the order we are delivering tomorrow to Bloomingdale's. I need everyone to stay late and finish the order so we can send it on the truck tomorrow. It's imperative we get this done for them." There was a groan as the women checked the clock and had to reassess their progress for the day. Mahala realized they would need another three hours to complete the order to Bloomingdale's specifications. It was not unusual for Mr. Koifman to stick these last-minute additions into the workflow—most women welcomed the extra money it would put into their paychecks—but it wasn't always easy to muster the stamina needed to continue to turn out a high-quality garment.

Mahala glanced up at Mrs. Leibowitz and saw that she looked worn down. The circles under her eyes were darker. She limped along, moving slower than she had just an hour before. Her eyes looked heavy as she fed the fabric under the sharp needle. Mahala could hear her neighbor's machine's pace slow, then pick up, as if she were losing concentration or alertness, her foot lightening on the pedal.

"*Oy Gutt!* I did it again!" Mrs. Leibowitz swore. Mahala looked over in time to see blood dripping down her fingers. Mrs. Leibowitz reached into the basket she kept under her worktable for some cotton to stop the blood flow, careful not to get any drops on the dress she was sewing.

"Mrs. Leibowitz! Are you okay? That looks deep." Mahala jumped up and came to her side. She took her injured hand in her own and examined it. The needle had not gone straight in but instead snagged and ripped the side of her finger. It was much worse than her previous injuries.

"I . . . I have to finish . . . The deadline . . . it's coming."

"You may need a doctor to stitch that up for you."

"No, bubbeleh, I'll be okay. I don't want to make a fuss. Mr. Koifman will be mad enough." She wrapped her injured finger in the cotton.

"Are you kidding? This happened because Mr. Koifman is making us work too long! This stops now!"

"No, Mahala," Mrs. Leibowitz begged, "please don't complain because of me. I'm clumsy. It was my fault."

"No. It was Mr. Koifman's fault!" Mahala turned on her heel and marched directly to his office, determined to put an end to this. She swung the door open on its hinges so quickly it crashed into the shelves that lined his office. Startled, Mr. Koifman fumbled with his pen, then set it down on his desk on top of the papers he had been working on.

"What do you mean by barging in here like that, young lady?" He looked her directly in the eye with an intense stare.

"Mr. Koifman, this has gone too far and it needs to end. Mrs. Leibowitz just sewed over her finger and is bleeding like a stuck pig! According to our union we should have been done with the workday two hours ago! You run this place like a tyrant, but I'm not afraid of you!" Mahala returned his stare. "I'm reporting you to the union. People are getting hurt. These working conditions are not acceptable. You've intimidated and manipulated the women here into doing what is best for you and your company while you bully the women into giving up what they rightfully have earned. They have earned the right to have breaks and to do what they want on those breaks, even if you think that smoking is a disgusting filthy habit. Keep your opinions to yourself. It's none of your business." Mahala's voice was clear and forceful. "And we are closing up shop at six o'clock sharp without fail. You will have to tell the department stores that they need to adjust their expectations of our production and delivery." Mahala paused to take a breath and realized she'd said her piece.

"How dare you take that tone with me," Mr. Koifman shot back. "This is *my* business and I'll run it as I see fit. I could fire you for your insubordination, Mahala."

Koifman paused and considered her. She held his gaze. "I'm sure it's not as bad as you think," he said brusquely. He picked up the stack of papers, tapped them lightly on his desk, and set them down again. "You can't always threaten to go to the union when things don't go perfectly."

"I'm not threatening, I'm informing you. I will be calling our union leader tonight to report this incident." As she swept out of the room, she knew he was calculating the fines he would be subject to when this was reported.

Following her visit to the ILGWU's headquarters, Mahala brought the full strength of the union down on Mr. Koifman. She got what she wanted from him—which was just to be treated fairly. She became the unofficial spokesperson for the ladies of the shop. They made requests through her because she was successful at getting results. It got to be that Mr. Koifman would cringe a little when he saw Mahala approaching his office with a determined look in her eye.

She tacked a copy of the contract on the shop wall at the entrance to the break room. Mysteriously, it went missing several times. No one owned up to removing it, but it was obvious to Mahala that Mr. Koifman had one of his minions pluck it off the wall, or perhaps the man himself did the deed. It made no difference; Mahala kept up the pressure. She made sure to strictly adhere to the contract, so that she would have the power of the union to back her up when needed. Although she was working a full-time job at the garment factory, she made it a priority to be part of the ILGWU administration. Not only did she faithfully attend union shop meetings, she also visited the ILGWU headquarters to network with the leader there. On her subway rides home, she couldn't help but wonder how her fathers' lives in the sugarcane factory might've been different—safer, better paid, less fragile—if its workers had unionized.

Mahala finished cleaning up her workstation and glanced over at Ruby to check her progress. "I'm headed downtown tonight. I know it's late, but do you want to join me?" Mahala asked.

"I can't," Ruby said, grimacing. "Jerome will be home soon. I need to get dinner on the table."

"Okay," Mahala responded, taking care not to push her friend. "I'll catch up with you later tonight." She gathered her coat and bag and walked to Times Square, where she took a bus down to ILGWU headquarters on Waverly Place.

The meeting came to order and started with a review of the minutes from the previous month's meeting and a reading of the agenda. Next, the chairman stood and addressed those assembled. "More than a decade ago, the Cloakmakers' Strike broke and set new precedent for an array of changes we're proud of, establishing our standard fifty-hour work week as well as overtime pay. But we have more to accomplish in order to protect and establish the rights of our members. Efforts at negotiations are of paramount importance." He swung his hand up into the air.

"We must strive to keep our members safe. We all know the physical dangers of strikes—some of us from firsthand experience. We've seen striking workers get assaulted with no one there to protect them, hurt by thugs hired by ruthless business owners willing to pay off the police to look the other way."

Mahala felt a cold shiver go down her spine as she listened intently.

"It is time for a new strategy," the chairman insisted. "I'm talking about the power of information. We need to make it clear that we are not greedy, but rather we want to be partners in the company's success. In order to do that, we need better working conditions."

The seven union leaders nodded in agreement.

"There has been an effort from business owners to ask for arbitration to settle our differences. I know a lot of you think that going to trial reduces our power, but I think we need to be prepared if the courts give them the power to do that. I'm calling on local leaders. I need all of you to work your territory and get the documentation—on factory conditions, on wages, on health concerns—that we need for a courts-focused strategy. Can I count on you?" He raised his eyebrows and lifted one hand, palm side up, beseechingly to the members in the room.

Inspired by his words, Mahala was one of the first to raise her hand to volunteer.

When she returned to work the following morning, she saw everything with new eyes. The bins that held the discarded remnant scraps had a cloud of dust floating above them, coating the floor with fine particles. The sewing machines themselves gave off dust as the needles pierced the soft fabric thousands of times each minute. The cutters were practically cocooned in it, their scissors flashing as they cut out and piled the pieces around themselves, awaiting the runners to distribute their work to the seamstresses. They were all breathing that dust into their lungs every day.

But that wasn't all. Pins were scattered across the floor, making it as slippery as glass. The air was hot due to poor ventilation and clogged, dusty air ducts—which themselves posed a fire hazard.

As she started talking with her coworkers, Mahala realized that many of them did have trouble breathing on the factory floor. She thought about how many times she made trips to the break room to down a glass of water to soothe her parched throat. Drinks of any sort were forbidden on the floor for the potential damage they might do to the garments they were manufacturing—but what about the potential damage that fainting from heat and dehydration might do to the workers?

Mahala asked the ladies about where they lived, what they paid in rent, and where their husbands worked. She probed their ability to pay their bills and if they ever found themselves unable to make ends meet. Most of the women freely gave her the information, but some were reluctant to share the details of their financial situations. Mahala was careful not to alienate these women. She wanted to make it clear that she was interested in helping them—she wanted them as allies.

CHAPTER 34
Mahala

Mahala blinked her eyes open. It was mid-December in Manhattan, and temperatures outside and in were icy cold. A shiver went through her body as she reached for her heavy robe with one hand and massaged her sore neck with the other. Sleeping on the sofa sometimes left her achy first thing in the morning, but it was nothing she couldn't handle. Ruby and Jerome kept the apartment cool in an effort to be economical, which Mahala completely understood, grateful that she was still welcome in their home. She had assumed that she would have a place of her own by now, but Ruby had insisted she stay with them to continue saving money.

Mahala parted the curtains to the living room window and noticed small icicles hanging from the top of the window. Frost clung to the windowpanes, providing a delicate lacy outline on the glass. She enjoyed the change of seasons in New York, but she missed the balmy temperatures of St. Vincent.

It was Saturday morning. She and Ruby would be finished with work slightly earlier than weekdays, so they would have time to prepare to go out for the evening. The two friends and Jerome were in the habit of frequenting the Portuguese Club on Saturday nights to socialize and entertain themselves. Many people from both St. Vincent and the smaller island of Bequia were members of the club since both islands had a large Portuguese population. The club had a band that played both ragtime and jazz music, which they all found fun, upbeat, and easy to dance to. Mahala had been asked to dance many times, but no one gentleman caught her eye.

Just after supper that evening, Mahala changed into her newest gray chiffon dress with a drop waist drape and side bow, pulling down the matching cloche hat from its home atop her makeshift wardrobe and sliding her feet into strappy sharkskin shoes.

"Pass me the pearls, will you?" she asked Ruby, who was struggling with the asymmetrical bow on the shoulder of her own navy dress. "Wait, here, let me help." She smoothed the bow and straightened the long white triangle applique cascading from Ruby's shoulders to just below her waist.

"Thanks," Ruby said, reaching into her closet and looping a long string of faux pearls over Mahala's neck. The strand reached well below her natural waist.

"Wow, you ladies look radiant!" Jerome beamed as they collected their handbags and tugged on their coats and gloves. "I'm proud to escort you both tonight." He bent both his elbows, offering one arm to each lady.

As they approached the entrance to the club, they could hear the band's ragtime music pulsing through the doors, inviting them to join the energy of the club. Inside, several men were lined up in front of the refreshment table, sampling the nonalcoholic punch. The club members were very careful not to break the Prohibition laws. It wasn't worth the risk of being shut down by the authorities. No one seemed to mind the absence of cocktails as long as the band kept the atmosphere lively.

Mahala chatted with Ruby while listening to the band swing and jive. She smoothed the edges of her long hair, which had been tucked under and pinned to resemble a bob. Ruby was always telling her she'd look marvelous with it short, but she was not ready to shear her silky mane.

"Would you care to dance?" a low voice asked. Mahala turned, surprised to find that a handsome gentleman had approached her. He was not tall, but still stood well over her five-foot one-inch height. His dark hair was cropped tight and parted on the side, longer on top, revealing a slight wave. He had the appearance of a man recently discharged from the military, his muscular physique evident through his dark three-piece suit. Working in the fashion industry had given Mahala a discerning eye for detail; now, she noticed he wore a double-breasted vest, topped with a single-breasted suit jacket with a high lapel—undoubtedly an imitation but still a nice look.

"Well?" he said warmly. He had both arms resting behind his back and tipped his head slightly to the right as he waited for her reply.

"I would be delighted," Mahala said, smiling. The gentleman extended his hand palm side up and waited for Mahala to place her fingers in his. He led her to the dance floor and placed a firm hand on the small of her back. He moved in perfect rhythm to the fast beat, alternately releasing and increasing the tension on Mahala's lower back as he led her in a foxtrot. They moved into the second song before he spoke again.

"You're a wonderful dancer. I hate to say it, but sometimes you ask a girl to dance, and she can't follow a lead." He smiled and introduced himself. "I'm Ormond."

"I'm Mahala," she said, returning his smile. "And thank you for the compliment. I owe it all to my friend Ruby. We have practiced for years with each other at home."

"Mahala is such a beautiful and unusual name. I've never heard it before."

"Thank you. My parents are from India, and they named me after the Taj Mahal. They were both in awe of its beauty and magnificence, they said." She tipped her head slightly. "It's a lofty namesake to live up to."

"It fits you perfectly." He winked at her and spun her around his back, catching her hand delicately on the other side.

Several songs later, they left the dance floor laughing in search of a glass of punch. Mahala and Ormond began to share some details about their lives with each other. To her delight, she discovered that his family lived in Bequia, part of the same island chain of St. Vincent and the Grenadines located just an hour ferry ride away from her home. They found they had much more in common than just their island home. Both of their families had made their way to the British West Indies Islands in pursuit of a better life. In turn, each of them had worked to improve their situation from that of their parents. An hour passed, and then another.

When she finally made eye contact with Ruby across the room, her friend was waving at them with Mahala's coat and handbag over her arm. "I've got to go, it seems," she said wistfully.

Ormond pulled a nub of a pencil from his breast pocket and took a paper menu from the table.

"Here," he said. "Let me take your address, or your telephone number if you've got a line. I'd love to see you again." Mahala nodded, scribbling Ruby's address in the dim light of the club. They parted with a smile, and as Mahala made her way across the room, Ruby's eyebrows already quirked with interest, she felt a blush creep up her cheeks.

Mahala and Ormond met the following week at the club. They danced again, this time to swing. They moved together as one, as if they had been dancing as partners their whole lives.

They had an instant connection with each other. Mahala appreciated Ormond's good looks but was attracted to his respectful attitude even more. He seemed genuinely interested in what was important to her. At thirty-three, he was ten years older than she and confessed that he was looking forward to settling down and starting a family. She wasn't bothered by the age difference in the least. Most women she knew were married to men a good deal older than themselves. She thought back through the catalogue of suitors her parents had tried to ply her with—and could practically hear Kavita's voice reminding her that that meant that they were old enough to be established in their careers and likely to be good providers for their future family when the children came along.

As he walked her back to the dance floor after a punch break, Mahala thought of how long she'd avoided any talk of marriage, any threat of commitment, even any hint of love if it meant tying her down to someone else's future. But now, with snow falling outside—snow! something she'd dreamed of seeing as a child—and Ormond's fingers pressed warmly beneath her shoulder blade, she thought perhaps it was time to open her heart at last.

Ormond invited Mahala on a date after two evenings at the social club. New Year's Eve was a week away, but it seemed like too much pressure for a first date, so they decided on the week after. Of course, as any true gentleman would, he offered to invite Ruby along if Mahala felt it necessary to have a chaperone. She scoffed, thinking of her journey to Panama and Jane's chaperone suggestions then, and agreed to meet him for dinner, just the two of them, if he picked her up at Ruby and Jerome's apartment.

When Mahala heard the buzzer in the living room ring, she made one last sweep of her face with her powder puff and freshened her crimson lipstick, blotting any excess on a tissue. She ran her hands along her intricately braided coiffure to check for any spots that had come loose and was satisfied that everything was obediently in place. She felt elegant in her cream-colored silk blouse and navy pleated skirt. From the living space came the sound of the door opening, low voices murmuring, and then Jerome calling her name. She checked her reflection one last time and glided into the living room to greet her suitor.

When Ormond caught a glimpse of her, he immediately sprang up from his chair—but waited for her to come closer. "Hello, Mahala." He smiled at her. "You look beautiful tonight."

"Thank you," she said with a wide smile and twinkle in her liquid brown eyes as she approached. "It's so nice to see you."

"I've made a reservation at a place called Divan Parisien. It's a French bistro. I've read about it in the newspaper. Apparently, *bistros* are common in Paris. You told me that you like new things, so I hope you'll like it."

"I'm sure I will. That was really thoughtful of you." She turned her head to see Ruby enter with a cup of tea.

After a few minutes of pleasant conversation, Ormond and Mahala departed for their date. Ormond offered his elbow for Mahala to hold onto as they walked the short distance down the sidewalk to the subway station. The restaurant was only two stops from the Govias' apartment. The short ride would give them time to sit close together before they were seated opposite each other in the restaurant. Despite the frigid temperatures, the subway car was warm, and the hum of the train moving along the tracks was relaxing. They chatted easily on the way to the restaurant. Ormond told Mahala that he had a good job as an electroplater. She assumed that meant he made a decent living, whatever that meant.

The train came to an abrupt stop, and Ormond looked through the window at the sign on the wall. "This is us," he announced.

They both jumped up out of their seats and exited the train before the doors snapped closed. They emerged from the subway and strolled, arms linked, down the sidewalk until they saw the restaurant.

They entered Divan Parisien and were greeted by the maître d', who whisked them over to their table for two. He pulled out the espresso-colored wicker chair for Mahala and gently pushed her in. Ormond seated himself and took in the ambiance. A silver bud vase with three pink carnations adorned the white starched linen tablecloth. Potted palms stood in each corner of the dining room. The leaves reminded Mahala of St. Vincent.

The maître d' handed Mahala a menu first, then Ormond, then stepped away to give them privacy. They both ordered the broiled supreme of bluefish, served with lyonnaise potatoes and creamed spinach. Ormond looked into Mahala's eyes the entire meal and barely finished his dinner. She felt the warmth of his gaze from her toes to her ears, glowing happily.

"So, you know what I do for work, but I still don't know what an electroplater *does*," Mahala said.

"An electroplater puts a metal coating on objects to make them appear shiny and more valuable. I work mostly with cutlery and jewelry." He reached across the table to take her hands in his.

"Basically, you dip the objects into a special chemical solution, then into the metal, and then run a current through it. That way, the metal gets deposited on the object."

"And then it's shiny?"

"No, not really. You have to buff it to get that nice mirror-like finish," Ormond explained.

Mahala was enjoying learning more about his expertise and the science of his work.

Over dinner, she found out that he had served in the United States Army in the Great War and was discharged in 1918. Although he hadn't served in over five years, he managed to keep himself in extremely good physical condition. Once their plates were cleared away, Ormond complimented Mahala on her beauty—something she was used to hearing, but it filled her with pride when *he* said it. He couldn't take his eyes off her.

After dessert of profiterole glace, they both noticed that they had been talking for more than three hours. They were the only patrons left in the restaurant. Mahala couldn't remember when she felt such a natural connection with—and attraction to—another person. Even Ben, sweet as he'd been, had never stirred these kinds of feelings. As Ormond walked her home through the bitter cold, Mahala felt like she was floating on air.

CHAPTER 35
Mahala

MAHALA AND RUBY RETURNED HOME from another day at Koifman's. Ruby grabbed the mail out of the box and began leafing through it as they ascended the stairs to the apartment. "Why is it that it's never anything but bills?" she sighed and continued flipping through the letters. She stopped at the fourth envelope. Mahala glanced over Ruby's shoulder and saw her mother's distinct handwriting spelling out her name. Ruby immediately turned to Mahala.

"I'm sure it's a Christmas greeting with lots of news of your nieces and plans for celebration!" She thrust the letter in Mahala's direction.

Mahala was always happy to open a letter from home. Despite her parents' threats never to speak with her again, she wrote frequently, assuring them that she was happy and well and that she loved them. She made a promise to herself that she would not cut them out of her life, even if they were angry with one another. Once every now and then, a letter from Sofia or Jane would come, reporting the household news.

Her mother's beautiful handwriting was a welcome sight to Mahala's eyes. As she read on, her smile quickly faded, and her brows knit with worry.

Jane Simons
Ratho Mill, St. Vincent VC0274
Dear Mahala,

Unfortunately, I have bad news to report. Papa has fallen ill. I'm afraid that it may be too late by the time you receive this letter, but I pray that he still has time. The doctor says he's had another heart attack. He's in the hospital and he's been asking for you. If you can find a way back home to us, he would be so happy, and I would be grateful to you. Please make haste! You belong here in St. Vincent, your true home.

Your loving Mama

Mahala's stomach instantly tightened into knots. Her mind raced with the arrangements she would have to make to return to St. Vincent. She could book passage on the next ship to Barbados, but it would take five days and then she would need to take the ferry the rest of the way. Her father had to make it until she arrived. He just had to.

Koifman's was another matter altogether. Mr. Koifman would not be happy about her leaving for an indefinite amount of time, especially during the busiest time of the year. They still had mountains of dresses to finish, and then they would immediately start on the spring orders. She would have to hope that her loyal service and quality workmanship would convince him to hold her job for her until she returned.

Ruby interrupted her thoughts. "Mahala, is everything all right? You look as pale as a ghost."

"No, Papa—Papa is in the hospital recovering from a heart attack, and Mama is imploring me to return home at once," she whispered. "I have to go. He's asking for me—I have to go to him. I've already lost one father, I can't lose another without having a chance to say goodbye." Mahala hurriedly tucked the letter back into the envelope and swept into their shared apartment. Ruby followed after her, set her belongings down on the hall table, and started to rattle off her own list of things that needed to be done for Mahala's journey.

When Mahala arrived at work the next day, she immediately went in to see Mr. Koifman, rushing into his office without knocking.

"I'm sorry, but I have to go see my father in St. Vincent. He's very ill, and I need to leave immediately. I feel terrible because I know we are really busy and have tons of orders—" Her voice cracked, a lump forming in her throat.

"I'm so sorry. It sounds very serious." Mr. Koifman cut off her explanation.

Mahala gaped at him through the sting of tears. "But what about my work? . . . Aren't you mad?"

"My mother had cancer a few years ago. I dropped everything to be by her side. I was lucky to have my brother-in-law to cover for me with the business." He walked out from his desk and took her hand in his and gently patted it. "It was advanced when they found it, so it was quick. Go . . . you should be with him. Jobs are replaceable; people aren't."

"Thank you." It was all Mahala could manage. She spun on her heels and whipped out of his office before he had a change of heart.

CHAPTER 36
Mahala

St. Vincent, British West Indies

MAHALA DISEMBARKED FROM THE FERRY in St. Vincent and got a ride directly to the Simons house to see her father. It had been ten days since she received her mother's shocking letter. The only word she'd had since was a brief note that intercepted her just before her departure: while the heart attack had been major and left him weakened, John was now convalescing at home. Mahala was glad to be spared from entering the hospital—a place that held such painful memories for her of Ganesh's fatal injury.

Mahala gently cracked the front door and went lightly into John's bedroom—even though what she really wanted to do was to launch herself at him like a catapult. As anxious as she was to see him, she didn't want to startle him. Relief flooded over her when she saw his smiling face glancing up at her in the doorway.

"My sweet Mahala," he whispered in a breathy exhale. He reached his hand up, beckoning her to his side. She took up his hand in both of her own and kissed him lightly on his cheek.

"Papa, I'm so glad you're feeling better." She rubbed his arm. "I was so worried when I got Mama's letter."

"Hush. You're here now. That's what matters." Jane's voice surprised her—just as her mother's arms wrapped around her shoulders from the back in a warm hug. Mahala hadn't noticed her come in. John's eyes flickered to Jane behind her and then to his bedside table. She responded to his wordless request, releasing Mahala and coming around the left side of the bed, lifting his head to bring the glass of water to his lips. Jane returned the glass to the table, then settled his head back on his pillow and motioned to Mahala to follow her. John slowly closed his eyes and drifted off to a peaceful sleep.

Mahala hurried after Jane to the living room. "Mama, what does the doctor think? Will he be okay, or is he still in danger?"

"There is no guarantee, of course," Jane sighed, sinking into the settee, "but they think there is a good chance that he will recover. This is his second heart attack, and it was more serious than the first. They said in many cases rest and oxygen, as well as aspirin, will speed the recovery process. There was nothing more they could do for him at the hospital that I couldn't do for him more comfortably at home. The doctor comes every few days to give him oxygen, so it's easier for him to breathe. He's getting stronger but he's still not supposed to get out of bed other than to use the bathroom. For once, he's following a doctor's advice." She allowed a small smile to cross her face.

Mahala was somewhat relieved—Jane seemed to be handling this well. "What is he doing about the sugar mill? Does he have someone he trusts to look after things?"

"You know Papa, everything works like a well-oiled machine down there. He's trained several apprentices to do things his way, and they come and give him updates. He's not supposed to worry about business right now, but of course he can't get himself to stop."

"That sounds like Papa." She looked around, suddenly realizing that the house was very quiet. "Where are my nieces?"

"I sent them to Elizabeth's house after school. I thought there would be too much excitement in the house when you came. You know how much they love you. They'll squeal like happy little piglets when they catch sight of you. You'll see them later if you join us for dinner. I'm assuming that is your plan."

"Of course! I just want to say hi to Mai first. You and Papa are my priority." She picked up a glass of water from the tray Jane had set out for her earlier and took a sip. "Is Henry planning on coming?"

"I don't know yet." Jane tightened her lips.

Mahala shook her head, grinding her teeth. "Mama, I'm worried about what his absence is doing to Sofia and Lily. Does he really expect you to raise them permanently?"

"They're more grown up every day. Wait until you see them. They remind me of you at that age." Jane moved a book over an inch to the right and the candy dish an inch back toward the center of the coffee table and brushed the surface of imaginary crumbs.

"Mama, he's still giving you excuses."

"He visits them when he can get time off from work. His new wife is overwhelmed with the baby, and she doesn't want his older children adding to the chaos."

"They're *his* children," Mahala exclaimed. "Does he really think that he can hide them away here forever? They lost their mother."

"Shhhhh . . . you'll wake your father." Jane's eyes glanced at the bedroom door where John slept.

"They need their father to claim them, to love them, to *want* them," Mahala hissed. "What's wrong with him? Is he really that selfish?"

"I *know*, I'm going to work on it. It's just . . . it's just that they need me now more than ever." She reached for her daughter's arm and gave her a squeeze. "Come, let's talk about more pleasant things."

Mahala knew this wasn't going to get solved any time soon because Jane always gave Henry the benefit of the doubt. She relented and allowed her mother to go on.

"I'm so happy to have you home, sweetheart. I've missed you terribly. You'll make arrangements to send for your things?"

"I've brought what I need with me Mama." She motioned to her valise.

"Oh, I know you have your small case, but what about the rest of your things? Surely, you've made arrangements to ship them home?"

"No, Mama, I haven't," Mahala said slowly. She moved to sit closer to Jane, reaching for her hand. "I don't think you understand. I'm not coming home permanently. I live in New York. That's where my life is now."

Jane's expression dropped. "But—but your father and I need you here, now more than ever."

"I'm not moving back. I'm here for Papa, but my life is in New York. I thought you understood." Her eyes narrowed at her mother's confusion. She tried to think of a way to make Jane understand. "I . . . I didn't want to tell you like this, but I—I've also met someone there. It's just the beginning, but I really like him. His name is Ormond Marks, and he is actually from Bequia." Her voice went up slightly along with her eyebrow. "He is waiting for me back home—in New York, I mean."

"What kind of name is Marks? Is he Indian?" Jane queried with a glimmer of hope.

"No, his family is Portuguese. The original spelling of his family name was M-a-r-q-u-e-s, but they anglicized it when they immigrated. I do think that the former was more elegant," Mahala explained. "You should be happy—he's a war veteran, gainfully employed, very polite, and ever the gentleman. He's a wonderful dancer and *very* handsome. But his looks are not what drew me to him. I find him so easy to talk to and I like how much his family means to him. He sends money home to his family in Bequia and is very close to his brother and sister. I admire his integrity and—" She paused, realizing she'd been on the cusp of saying "and his family values" but knew that Jane would immediately ask her about the possibility of children.

"Mahala, aren't you afraid that going around town with a man you hardly know, not to mention unchaperoned, is a bit scandalous?"

"Mama, I'm almost twenty-four years old! I don't need anyone's permission to be courted any longer," Mahala huffed, a little more forcefully than she had intended. She reminded herself why she was in St. Vincent. She did not want to get embroiled in the same tired debate of who she should marry. "Let's change the subject."

"All right, my sweet," Jane said reluctantly, "you're probably exhausted from your travels. Why don't you go say hi to your mother, freshen up a little, and both of you come back here for dinner? We can visit quietly with Papa and your nieces. Do you want me to make up Henry's room for you so you can stay here and be close to Papa?"

"Okay, but I just want to make sure that Mai's feeling aren't hurt that I'm not staying at home with her."

The following day, Mahala received a visitor of her own. She answered the door to find Ben standing there with a bouquet of wildflowers.

"What a surprise!" Mahala exclaimed as she accepted the bouquet. She wrapped her other arm around him in a warm hug. Ben stepped in and removed his hat.

"It's been a while, hasn't it? Those are from my pop's garden. My mother told me about your papa. How's he doing?" He followed her to the kitchen. Mahala opened a few cabinet doors before she found the right one where her mother kept several vases. She plucked a medium-sized one off the shelf.

"He's recovering and taking it easy, which is a hard thing for John Simons to do." She filled the vase with water from the tap and dropped the flowers in, readjusting the stems to spread them out evenly. She placed them on the table.

"It sounded serious, the way my mother described it," Ben said.

Mahala nodded. "I'm worried about him. He's not good at functioning at half speed."

"It's good that you're here for him. I'm glad you came too."

"Me too," Mahala smiled at Ben. "It means a lot to me that you're here."

Ben returned several days in a row and Mahala took refuge in his company. When she woke her first thought was her father and her second was Ben. This morning when she greeted him at the door, he looked as if he was on a mission. His eyes were clear and focused on her. "Hey, what do you say to a little change of scenery today?"

Mahala took a step back, opening the door for him, and Ben followed her inside. She glanced up at the clock. "Well—I—I don't really want to . . ."

Ben reached for her hand. "We won't be gone long. I promise."

She turned toward John's bedroom. "Let me just check on Papa first." She slipped out of his grip, tiptoed to John's door and stole a look inside, then pivoted back toward Ben. "He's still asleep, and Mama's next door, so I guess it will be all right." She followed Ben's lead and came to his side. Once they were out the door, their strides synchronized. "Hey, are you sure that it's okay for you to be away from work this much?"

"I know the boss," he said with a wink. "Pop is picking up the slack for me. He's still got it, that old guy." He smiled easily and extended his elbow for her as she navigated the dirt path.

"I don't want to monopolize your time."

"Come on, Mahala, it's me you're talking to. Other than work, I don't have anything else going on. You're my priority . . . I mean, while you're here." He cleared his throat.

"I'm glad you're forcing me to get out of the house." They walked in comfortable silence until they arrived at the park where they used to picnic. Ben sat down on a rock in the clearing and swept his hand over the space next to him, inviting Mahala to join him. "It's good to see you," Ben said, turning to face her. "I wish the circumstances were different, but . . ." She touched the side of his arm. "I missed you too." She smiled. "And your sense of humor. You always know the right thing to say to lift my mood."

"It's one of my many talents," he said playfully.

They chatted for a few minutes and just as she felt her mind begin to relax, her thoughts snapped back to John. She checked her watch. "Would you mind if we headed back?" She slid down the rock and stood up. Ben sprang up. "Sure I—I hope I was able to get your mind off things a bit."

"It was just what I needed." She started walking, waiting until he was at her side before quickening her pace to return to John. During the walk back, Mahala realized that Ben had stirred up old feelings in her that she was confused about. He didn't confess his love to her this time, but he made it clear that there was nobody else currently in his life.

Five days later, Mahala awoke to the sound of screaming. An animal outside, she wondered foggily—but no, a person, a woman. *Jane.*

Mahala leaped from her bed, nearly tripping over her valise, and dashed out of Henry's room down the hall. Flinging open her parents' bedroom door, she found Jane curled around John's still form.

"I woke for a glass of water," she sobbed. "He was already gone."

Mahala buried a father for the second time in her short life. Her heart was heavy with grief for herself and for her mother. Henry arrived for the funeral but announced that he had only two days before he had to return to Panama. Mahala bristled at his callousness, shocked by the haste with which he would speed back to life with Carolina and leave his grieving daughters behind. Even Elizabeth, always proper and kind, glowered at him when he told them. Yet even he clearly felt his father's loss, and Mahala couldn't help but feel like they were united in missing John.

After the funeral, back home, Mahala wrapped her arms around Jane and whispered, "I loved Papa so much my heart aches. I just can't believe he's gone."

"He—he was doing so well. He was following the doctor's orders . . ." Jane trailed off.

Mahala looked through the window to her nieces in the garden. Lily pushed Sofia on the swing, struggling to move her big sister's weight. "Poor girls. They are losing more than just a grandfather . . . It makes me so angry when I think what Henry did to those girls."

Jane's eyes widened and she glanced at Henry across the room, talking with neighbors. "He did the best he could," she whispered woodenly.

"No, he didn't, Mama," Mahala snapped, grief for her own father fueling anger at her brother's failings as one. "He's fallen far short of being a good father to them. He could have taken them back to Panama when Violet died. He could have integrated them into his new family. He could have demanded that his new wife accept them. He didn't do any of those things. Instead, he left all the hard work to you and Papa."

Jane blinked. "He has a very demanding job as a doctor, Mahala."

"That's just an excuse. Lots of people have demanding jobs and they still can be parents. Papa was. Henry took the easy way out and you let him." She looked over in Henry's direction. "Look at him. He's abandoning those girls again tomorrow."

Jane stood speechless. Mahala could see that she had probably said too much. She decided to retreat. They were all suffering with fresh grief.

Mahala spotted Ben across the room and was grateful for his support during her time on the island. He was a welcome bright light in the gloom that she felt.

CHAPTER 37
Mahala

New York City

MAHALA RETURNED TO NEW YORK emotionally drained but ready to throw herself into her work. As she flagged down a cab, she thought about how she needed to see Mr. Koifman. She hoped she still had a job. Mr. Koifman had seemed to understand why she had to leave, but would he allow her to reclaim her position? Dusk was falling outside as they crept along the streets. She longed to see Ormond. Ruby had written to say that he had called on the Govias several times while Mahala was away, inquiring whether they'd heard from her, asking how she was, leaving several personal notes for her in Ruby's care.

To her surprise and delight, he was waiting outside the apartment, flowers in hand. He handed her the small bouquet, removed his hat, and gently reached for her hand, holding it lightly in his broad palm. Mahala could feel the warmth of his ungloved hand radiating in her own, and her heart quickened slightly.

"Mahala, I'm so very sorry about your father. You and your family have my deepest condolences. I know you loved him very much." His brown eyes locked onto hers. Her gaze fell to his. "Thank you," Mahala managed to reply. "Won't you come in?"

∞

After reconnecting with Ormond, Mahala was now intent on getting her job back. She had experienced an unexpected display of empathy from Mr. Koifman when she told him about her father's grave condition. She could only hope that there was a shred of that left in him now. She walked into Mr. Koifman's office and spoke from her heart. "Mr. Koifman, I know you don't owe me anything and I didn't expect you to hold my position open, but I would greatly appreciate it if you gave me the opportunity to work for you again." Mahala took a deep breath, bracing for his answer.

Mr. Koifman looked up, still holding his paperwork. "Business is business, Mahala." He cleared his throat. "I've been shorthanded since you left," he grumbled. He went back to studying his papers. Mahala stood still for a beat. Did he mean what she thought? Was the job hers once again? "What are you waiting for? Get going! We have orders to fill!" he barked. She dashed out of his office before he could change his mind.

∞

Mahala poured her energy into her work to mitigate her grief. Koifman still demanded long hours six days a week, but she still made time to see Ormond when she had time off on Saturday night or Sunday afternoon.

On Sunday evenings, she was in the habit of writing to her family—and even to Henry every few months, despite the fact that things were a bit strained between them. He was still her brother, and she hoped that they could get back the closeness they once had shared. Even if Henry made that difficult with his utter selfishness, she was determined to try. She wrote of the things she was accomplishing at work and her involvement in the union. After a bit of deliberation, she told him that she had met someone—a man—in New York, who was originally from Bequia. She didn't tell him that it was serious. But the telegram from him shortly after she posted her letter showed he'd guessed the truth.

Mahala, received your news. stop. Do not do anything. stop. Do not accept his proposal. stop. I have many doctor friends in New York. stop. Will find a suitable husband for you. stop. Will be in New York next month. stop.

Mahala held the telegram in her shaking hands. "He still thinks he can tell me what to do," she shouted. "Ormond didn't even propose yet."

"I suppose he's the head of the family now that John is gone. Don't you think that you should at least consider discussing it with him?" Ruby asked.

Mahala looked at her, aghast. "No, I don't care what he thinks, especially about my marital plans. You of all people should know that—it's why I'm here in New York instead of trapped on St. Vincent or in his precious Panama."

Ruby raised an eyebrow. "I know, but remember, this is Henry we're talking about. He's careful to avoid what's unpleasant in his own life but not shy about interfering in yours."

CHAPTER 38
Henry

Colon, Panama

HENRY WAS IRRITATED BY MAHALA'S latest letter. This situation with her Ormond fellow would have to be investigated. He sent some inquiries to his New York contacts. He was able to find out only that Ormond Marks was an electroplater by trade, an honorably discharged war veteran, and had lived his early years on the island of Bequia. Henry remembered that one of his classmates from medical school had a father who was a diplomat at the Panama consulate in New York. He promptly phoned him and asked for a favor. The resulting background check came up clean. Henry couldn't find any flaws other than the most obvious, which was that Ormond was a man of very modest means. He didn't want his sister doomed to a life of poverty if she ended up marrying Ormond. Henry understood how fast these matters could move; he had entered swiftly into marriage himself both times. With a woman as beautiful as Mahala, any man would be motivated to propose quickly.

Henry's next thought was to contact his colleague, Robert Chapman. Rumor had it that he was on the hunt for a wife. Henry had met Robert a few years ago at a medical convention. Robert had let it slip that he came from an extremely wealthy family, but unfortunately, he would not have access to his trust fund until he was both at least thirty-five and married. Robert had expensive tastes and did not hide the fact that he had amassed a sizable debt. He had a penchant for purchasing Italian-designed, custom-made suits and luxury Swiss watches. He had a collection of several luxury watch brands including a prized Patek Phillipe, which Henry coveted. The rate at which Robert spent money surely meant that he had to unlock his trust fund fast. Henry called him to discuss the possibility of coming to a mutually beneficial agreement.

CHAPTER 39
Mahala

New York

Mahala warned Ormond about her brother Henry's disapproval but assured him that she was her own woman and was capable of living her own life. What she didn't share was that she had seen Ben when she was in St. Vincent.

When Mahala thought about Ben, she remembered how effortlessly they understood each other and had developed an easy shorthand that required few words. She enjoyed his company immensely. But was this love? She didn't have the answer to that. Mahala also had strong feelings for Ormond. She didn't know if it was possible to be in love with two men simultaneously.

What she really couldn't confess to Ormond was that since her return, Ben had begun to write to her. She enjoyed hearing about how his business was going and the news about his parents. His letters started to take a more serious tone when he asked her to consider returning to the island. When she thought about his request, she felt a flush of guilt and refocused herself on work, reminding herself why she had made this decision to leave St. Vincent in the first place.

One Monday morning a few weeks later, Mahala and Ruby arrived at work early. As they neared Mr. Koifman's office, Mahala saw the light already on inside. This was not unusual, but there was someone else in there with him—which at this hour *was* unusual. Mahala noticed the gentleman was tall, almost too big for the suit he was wearing. His muscles strained at the fabric, bunching his sleeves up at the biceps instead of lying flat in a smooth line to the wrists. He didn't look like any of the usual people that visited Mr. Koifman. Most times there were shop boys, fabric cutters, work men, and designers, who were either in uniform, coveralls, or cotton shirts with their sleeves rolled up. This man was out of place.

Just then the man turned abruptly and left the office, coming face to face with Mahala. He looked at her and gave her a sly smile.

"Careful, doll, I hear the floor is slippery. I wouldn't want a beautiful thing like you to take a tumble and get hurt." He punctuated his gravelly words with a wink and turned the corner to leave the building.

Mahala wasn't sure what she had just witnessed. She saw beads of sweat at Mr. Koifman's temple through the open doorway. "Everything all right, Mr. Koifman?" she asked her boss.

"Yes . . . just fine. Good morning." He quickly picked up the orders on his desk.

Ruby tapped Mahala's arm and pointed toward the carts already filled with fabric that had been cut and needed to be pinned. *Right.* They worked at a fast pace all through the morning and had little conversation until their designated break.

At noon, Mahala and Ruby bounded into the cramped lunchroom. They gobbled down their leftovers from the previous night's dinner and downed large glasses of water. They could hardly rid their throats of the chronic dryness from the fabric particle dust constantly hanging in the air. Mahala perused the bulletin board for rentals—the thought of moving out of Ruby and Jerome's living room was always on her mind—but didn't see anything posted.

Just then Mr. Koifman walked in. His mouth was set in a straight line.

"Ladies, I know I have already put you off from last Friday's pay day, but it's going to be another day," he said evenly. "I'm sorry. I'm still waiting on receivables from some key accounts."

Mahala and Ruby exchanged a look. This was happening more frequently than the employees were comfortable with, but they had little recourse. They all needed the job, and they knew that he couldn't manufacture the money. However, they had put in many hours of hard work. They deserved to get paid—indeed, they *needed* to be. Most of them lived from paycheck to paycheck with no savings, so they depended on getting the money they were due on time. Jerome had had to cover her expenses over the weekend, since neither girl had been paid yet. Although the union contract had heavy fines for late payment of payroll, there was little to be done if the employer didn't have the funds.

"Who are you waiting on?" Mahala asked boldly.

"Bergdorf promised me a check this afternoon. I'm going over there to personally collect it," he snapped. He waltzed out, leaving Ruby and Mahala to finish their lunches in thoughtful silence.

∞

At home that night Mahala still felt that something wasn't quite right with Mr. Koifman's behavior—and it had something to do with that man that she had run into coming out of his office.

"I think that Mr. Koifman may have gotten himself involved with organized crime," Malala announced. She had heard the rumors of manufacturers being forced to take money from loan sharks or to make agreements with the mob in order to get cash quicker than applying for a bank loan. It was known that the trucking industry, which operated in and out the Garment District, was controlled by crime leaders.

"What? I can't believe Koifman would do that." Jerome's mouth gaped.

"Why do you think that?" Ruby asked.

"This was the third time in the last four weeks that we were asked to wait for our payday. It's obvious that Mr. Koifman has been having problems with cash lately. I don't know about his finances, but think about it—our orders go up and down with the seasons, fashion trends change on a dime, and we just successfully negotiated a pay raise in our piece rate. That means manufacturers are squeezed for cash. Koifman is no exception," Mahala explained.

"I read in the newspaper about that gangster, Luca Bianchi, controlling things in the Garment District, but I thought that was pro-union stuff," Jerome said.

"Like protecting union workers from getting beat up from the thugs that management hired? Yeah, but he also had his guys hand out beatings to management. He's a thug himself. He was rumored to have a price for breaking managers' thumbs and arms. I heard he even had a price for throwing a manager down an elevator shaft. I wouldn't put it past him to find a way to exploit management as well, if the price was right," Mahala said.

"They could definitely be playing both sides. Swoop in and supply much-needed cash to manufacturers when their lines falter or the season slows. Loan sharks charge some crazy high interest rates, though," Jerome said. "I don't know how the risk would be worth it. You'd have to be in pretty desperate straits."

"Seasonal ups and downs have always been part of the business," Ruby cut in.

"Of course, but what I'm saying is that Mr. Koifman was acting nervous and cagey and then there was the big guy that I didn't recognize—he could definitely be a loan shark," Mahala answered. "If Koifman's in trouble, that means we are, too."

"You both must be careful." Jerome turned to face his wife. "I don't want you getting too heavily involved in the union business. You could get hurt."

"I'm careful, I promise."

"We look out for each other." Mahala gently laid her hand on top of Ruby's and gave her a squeeze.

The next day, Mahala walked by Koifman's office and saw that his son had his arm in a sling tied close to his body. She slowed her pace, but accidentally made eye contact with him. The man frowned and closed the door, but the sound of their voices still traveled through the walls, which were entirely glass so that Mr. Koifman could view the whole floor from inside.

Mahala paused at a nearby cart and flipped through fabric swatches that she didn't need, straining to hear their muffled voices.

"Dad, he's insane. This is what he did to me when you were two days late."

"I'm sorry. I know. This was a huge mistake. I feel sick about it. It's only been going on a short time, I swear. I was desperate," Koifman pleaded with his son.

"Who's next if you don't pay him? My children, my wife?"

"No—hush, don't even say that. I'm done with it. This is the last time, I promise." He looked up and saw Mahala still hovering around his door and waved her away.

She hurried over to Ruby to tell her what she had heard, more afraid than ever.

It was out of her control who Mr. Koifman did business with. If it got bad or she felt threatened, she would have to consider looking for another job. That would mean starting at the bottom again and proving herself. Maybe a new boss would be far worse than Mr. Koifman. There were no guarantees.

CHAPTER 40
Mahala

A FEW WEEKS LATER, MAHALA was putting the finishing touches on a suit jacket when she saw Mr. Koifman waving to get her attention. He never liked to compete with the high-pitched hum of the sewing machines, preferring to talk in his office. Mahala set her work down and followed him. When she got close to his office, she paused with dread. Henry was sitting inside. Mr. Koifman stepped in front of her, blocking him briefly from view as he leaned in to be heard over the noise. "Your brother rattled my secretary just now, bursting through the doors and demanding to see you at once. He said it was urgent. Please make it quick and get back to work." Letting her pass inside, he then pulled the door closed and left them alone.

Mahala cleared her throat. "Hello, brother. Is everything all right? Mai, the girls?"

"Mahala, I'm here because I made a promise to Papa that I would take care of you."

She stiffened. "As you can see, I'm capable of taking care of myself."

"You think that marrying a penniless lovestruck fool will give you happiness for the rest of your life?" he said, glowering. "Is it honor or stubbornness that is guiding you into this decision? You'll doom yourself to a life of poverty. Look at you working in this sweatshop when a dignified lady would be at home taking care of her husband and family."

"Honest work is dignified, Henry. You taught me that yourself, working so hard."

"Yes, wonderful environment in here. I'm not sure if I enjoy my clogged throat or the ringing in my ears more."

"Your concern is touching, truly. After years of ignoring my pleas for more schooling despite seeing clearly that I was just as capable a student as you; after years of leaving me and Mama to raise your daughters while you made a new family, now suddenly I'm so important that you drop everything to intervene in my life?"

Henry stood and crossed the room to loom over her. "Mahala, I promised Papa that I would take care of you, and that means finding a suitable husband for you. I've arranged a meeting with a colleague of mine, a doctor who is also an eligible bachelor looking for a wife. He'll meet you tomorrow."

"That's completely unnecessary," she said evenly, moderating her voice to control her temper. "Where did you find him? Panama? I'm not leaving New York."

"He's from New York. He's doing research for Columbia Medical School in Washington Heights right in Manhattan, so he couldn't be closer. You'll meet him and you won't embarrass me," Henry commanded. Behind him through the glass, Mr. Koifman appeared, glaring impatiently.

Mahala glanced at her watch and realized if she didn't wrap this up, her boss's anger would reach the boiling point. Henry drew a breath, clearly ready to entrench for a drawn-out battle.

"All right, Henry." She turned on her heel as Mr. Koifman opened his door. Henry stood, towering over everyone, extending his hand for a handshake with her boss.

"Definitely forty-four extra-long," Mr. Koifman mumbled.

"Pardon me, did you say something?" Henry asked.

"Your jacket size. Hazard of the trade, I'm afraid."

Mahala rolled her eyes and swept out of the room. She'd take care of Henry's friend her own way. She always did.

CHAPTER 41
Mahala

MAHALA TRIED TO KEEP HER irritation with Henry in check as she dealt with his latest manipulation. In her opinion, most of the men Henry associated with were egotistical, overbearing, elitist doctors. Mahala had respect for the medical profession—there were certainly good doctors; indeed, Henry was one of them—but she knew that they were far from infallible. Her stomach tightened into knots when she thought about the fatal misdiagnosis her sister had received.

She focused her attention on what she would wear, what would say that she was respectable yet unavailable. An outfit was always like a puzzle, with all its separate pieces not making sense until they were brought together as a completed picture. Mahala made sure she was always well dressed no matter the occasion. The meeting with Henry's friend was no exception.

She selected a slate-gray, worsted wool dress with a square neckline and a wide, olive-green band at its dropped waist. Short white gloves accentuated her three-quarter length sleeves. To complete the outfit, she settled on a cloche in a slightly darker shade of gray and a matching gray wool coat. She checked her reflection in the mirror and was satisfied that she looked elegant and well groomed. She slipped her compact, lipstick, and wallet into her favorite drawstring bag, cinched it tight, and swung it on to her wrist.

She wasn't nervous about meeting this Robert Chapman fellow—she was just focused on getting it behind her. They had agreed to meet at a French café on Dyckman Street in the heart of Inwood—and in the middle of the day, instead of Saturday night. She didn't want him coming to call at Ruby's for fear this would seem far too much like a date. Ormond might get jealous.

She entered the café right on time and saw a man who could only be Robert already seated at a booth. He looked up when he heard the noise from the street roll in and rose out of his seat to greet her. Mahala noticed his elegant, perfectly cut charcoal suit, which he paired with a white cotton shirt and blue silk tie—an Italian design, she noted, as fashionable men were inclined to wear. His smooth brown skin glowed from a fresh shave. He pulled out her chair and invited her to sit down across from him.

Robert had taken the liberty of ordering an assortment of petits fours and tea. The silver tray was covered in the smallest iced cakes Mahala had ever seen. The mini confections were enrobed in chocolate and topped with delicate pink and white flowers.

They chatted politely for half an hour before the subject turned more serious.

"Your brother tells me that you're a tailor. How did you get into that?"

"I've always had skill with a needle and thread, and I love creating things." She didn't correct him when he said tailor instead of seamstress. Henry must've wanted to elevate her stature.

"Is it a by-product of being in the fashion business, or did you always have a gift for putting together the perfect ensemble?" He took in the full sight of her head to toe.

Mahala couldn't help feeling pride in her ability to dress herself well, despite her limited budget.

"I can see that you're a man who appreciates fine things," she said with a velvety voice. Up close, she noted the high quality of the fabric and construction of the suit he was wearing. She realized it was bespoke; definitely Italian-designed because of the high armholes, the narrow cut lapels, the more pronounced V-shaped torso of the jacket. She caught a glimpse of his elegant watch as he extended his arm to reach for his teacup. Everything about this man said elegance and sophistication.

"What about you? Do you teach, or do you practice medicine?"

"I practice, but I'm also working on a medical research project with colleagues at Columbia Medical School."

She smiled. "I remember the medical books Henry used to travel with. They were filled with pages and pages of illustrations and were heavy as a lead weight. He would point out the things that he thought I might find fascinating."

They chatted about his latest cases, the strangest things he'd seen as a doctor, how he liked living uptown. She enjoyed the tea and cakes he'd ordered. But she needed to be getting back. She wanted to see Ormond that evening.

"Mahala, would you have dinner with me tonight?" Robert interjected.

She hesitated before admitting, "Robert, I'm sure Henry didn't mention that I'm seeing someone. It's rather serious."

"You're not engaged to this fellow, are you?" he replied slowly.

"No, not yet."

"Good. Then there's no reason we shouldn't see each other again, is there?"

"I . . . I don't know." Mahala stammered. She didn't expect to be flustered by this friend of Henry's, but she found that, despite her initial resistance, she did appreciate his natural charm.

Robert looked her deeply in the eyes. "Your brother did not exaggerate; you are truly a remarkable and beautiful woman." He grinned.

"Thank you." Mahala returned his smile.

"May I be direct?" He raised an eyebrow.

"About what?"

"I could see myself with a woman like you. Can you see yourself with a man like me?"

She blushed. "We just met. We know nothing about each other."

"I know that I find you very attractive, and smart, and genuine."

"That's hardly enough."

"Why not? People have married for less."

Mahala was so unexpectedly caught up in Robert's charisma that she almost forgot that this was orchestrated by Henry—*almost*.

"It was nice to meet you, Robert. Thank you so much for the lovely conversation and the delicious tea." She rose out of her seat and picked up her coat. "I really must be going."

Robert took her coat from her and held it open. Mahala slipped one arm in as Robert wrapped her coat around for her. She grabbed her gloves and purse and glided toward the door with a smile. Robert instinctively opened the door for her.

"Bye. It was lovely meeting you too . . ." He trailed off as he watched her walk away.

On the subway ride home, she thought about her meeting with Robert. She couldn't deny that he was a rare find out of Henry's usual network of associates: charming, successful, and right here in New York. Despite her plans, it had proven difficult to be standoffish or rude to him; she wasn't sure she accomplished what she set out to. Guiltily, she concluded that, despite Henry's interference, she could have liked him—*did* like him, even.

When Mahala saw Ormond that night at the Portuguese Club, she worked up the courage to tell him about her meeting with Robert. After all, she'd reasoned, she didn't want it to feel like a big deal, something she needed to hide—and the only way to prevent it from feeling like a terrible secret was to prevent it from staying one.

"Henry set it up, you see. He lives in New York, just another doctor friend of his," she explained as they were dancing.

"Did he take you out?" Ormond's brows scrunched up.

"No. Well, yes . . . I guess so. I mean, I met him at a café for tea." She followed his lead as he stepped first with his left, then his right leg in a slow, slow, quick, quick pattern.

"Oh, I guess his wife didn't mind him meeting you?"

Mahala swallowed a knot in her throat, realizing she hadn't been clear. "He's not married."

Ormond's face flushed red, and he cleared his throat. He tightened his grip on Mahala's hand as they continued to foxtrot across the floor.

"Why are you suddenly so silent?" She felt his arms go rigid.

"Mahala, I—I just can't believe you're seeing other men. I thought we had something special here." He held her gaze.

"I'm not seeing other men," she replied, flustered.

"What would you call it, then?

"I've told you what Henry's like. He wouldn't have given up until I met with his friend." She registered the shock on his face. "I'm telling you because I wanted to be honest. My family will never stop trying to marry me off—"

He took a deep breath, raking his hand through his hair. "It's just—just—" He paused, an agonized look on his face, then silently led her out of the club to a secluded corner on the side alley.

"Please, Ormond, please, just talk to me. We can—" she began to plead, suddenly afraid of what his expression might mean, when he turned and pulled out a ring box.

"Mahala, I've been carrying this around all day. You make me so incredibly happy. I wanted to ask you to marry me tonight, but if Henry and your family will never accept me, if you're not sure . . ."

A pounding hum flooded Mahala's senses in panic, and her thoughts, inexplicably, flashed to Robert and Ben.

Robert, her brother's choice. A nice man in a nice suit with a nice job. A man she knew was looking for a *nice* wife, a wife like Henry's. A wife she could never be.

And Ben, dear Ben. She had received a letter from him just two days earlier, in which *he* declared his love for her and asked her to return to St. Vincent to be his wife. She couldn't lie; she did miss Ben as a friend, a special friend, someone who understood and respected her independence, who would no doubt be her two mothers' choice simply because he would lead her back home. Maybe if the timing were different, she could have considered a life with him.

She thought about all she had sacrificed to get here. She literally had no money when she arrived in New York, but she got a job and started building a career for herself and had her own income because of her perseverance. And it was that same perseverance that had led her to Ormond.

She felt her hand being squeezed, willed herself back to the present, and discovered Ormond had not pulled away, but gotten down on one knee. He looked at her, love and fear in his eyes. This man, she knew suddenly, this man was *her* choice. She could have her own life, her own future with this man—she loved him.

With a hesitant smile, Ormond said, "Mahala, I love you and I want to spend the rest of my life with you. Will you marry me?" He opened the box revealing a modest, yet beautiful diamond ring.

"Yes—yes, I will marry you." She pulled him up by the lapels, and he kissed her passionately. Laughing, they hurried back inside the club together. She fell more deeply in love with him as they danced and talked throughout the evening.

Eventually, she noticed the band starting to pack up their instruments and the staff sweeping up around them. "Oh, I didn't realize it was so late," Mahala said.

Ormond grinned, caressing her cheek. "I don't want tonight to end."

She returned his smile. "I know, neither do I, but I think these people are getting close to throwing us out." He put his arm around her, and they walked out beaming. "I can't wait to share our news with Ruby."

After saying goodnight to Ormond, Mahala tiptoed into the apartment in case Ruby and Jerome were asleep. She spotted Ruby, her robe pulled around her tightly, having a snack at the kitchen table. She joined her, unable to keep herself from grinning from ear to ear.

"Ormond proposed," Mahala announced. "I love him and there's really no reason to wait."

"Oh, Mahala, that's wonderful! I'm so happy for you," Ruby gushed. "Tell me everything!"

Mahala eagerly recounted the details of their proposal story, ending the happy tale with a sigh and eye roll. "Henry is bound to express his usual displeasure at my choice, but that's Henry."

"Do you think he'll make trouble for you or try to stop you from going through with it?"

She laughed. "Right now, geography is my friend."

"I have some news of my own," Ruby said. She swept the toast crumbs into a small pile on her placemat.

"Oh yeah, what's that?" Mahala took a bite of Ruby's buttered toast and washed it down with Ruby's glass of water.

"Well, it's . . . it's just that . . . I . . ." she stammered. "I'm going to have a baby. Jerome and I are going to be parents!"

"Oh Ruby, that's wonderful news! Congratulations. I'm so happy for you two." She pulled her friend in for a hug.

"Thanks, Mahala. You're not upset?" She raised her eyebrow.

"Upset?" She crinkled her nose and scrunched her brows. "Why would I be upset? Isn't that a natural part of being married?"

"Well yes, but I thought . . ."

"What?"

"Well, you know it's very tight quarters in this tiny apartment, and with a baby coming we'll be squeezed even tighter . . ." Ruby picked up the salt and pepper shakers and swept her hand under them before placing them back down in the same spot. "There isn't a spare inch in our bedroom for the cradle, so we don't have any choice but to put it out here in the living room."

"Once Ormond and I set a wedding date, we will have to make arrangements for our own apartment anyway. Unless you want me to look for a place to stay now?" Mahala asked. She hoped her friend was not in *too* much of a hurry to have her leave.

Ruby squeezed her hand. "It will be at least six months before the baby comes. Of course you can't move out now—I need your help to feather our nest. Jerome has nothing on your designer's eye."

"I'm going to write to Mai and Mama right away to let them know about my engagement. I know it may be hard for them, but they must accept the fact that I am committed to living in New York. Hopefully they will be happy for me."

CHAPTER 42

Henry

Colon, Panama

"HEN, SHE'S A TOTAL KNOCKOUT in the looks department, that's for sure," Robert told Henry, a little more flippantly than Henry would've liked. "I really liked her, but she seems rather involved with the fellow you mentioned." The phone line crackled as Robert exhaled.

"Look, this guy's a tradesman, you're a doctor—that trumps everything!"

"I'm not so sure. She didn't accept a second date from me, so I think she's really in love with this man of hers, despite what he does for a living. I don't want to sound callous, but it doesn't make sense to waste six months pursuing Mahala only to have her choose another man."

"It won't take that long. I guarantee it." Henry hoped that this was true. Robert had expressed his desire to unlock his trust fund numerous times. Henry couldn't help but feel proud of his own genius: he could stay true to the promise that he made to take care of his sister and do it in a way that would also be beneficial for his trusted friend. How could Mahala not see the logic and the practicality of marrying a wealthy man, or at least one that would be very wealthy shortly? They had both grown up poor; he'd scraped his way to the top by going to medical school and becoming a doctor, but Mahala didn't have that same opportunity—unless she listened to his advice and married well. She was too willful for her own good.

Henry contacted his sister the following day. He would have preferred to have this conversation with Mahala face to face but he didn't have time to travel back to New York, so a call would have to do. The Govias' apartment building didn't have a phone in the building. The only way to reach Mahala was to either call her at work or call the public pay phone in the drug store around the corner from the Govias' building. He begrudgingly knew Mr. Koifman would be irritated if he tried to interrupt Mahala's workday again, so he timed a phone call to the drug store and luckily, he got an amiable clerk to run around the corner to get his sister to come to the phone.

"Hello, Henry. This is a surprise."

"This is costing me a fortune, Mahala, so I'll be brief. You would be extremely lucky to marry a man like Robert Chapman. He's a good man and he would take care of you in style—"

"Ormond proposed," she cut in.

"You didn't accept, did you?" He spat the words back at her.

"I told him yes."

"Mahala, please don't do this," Henry implored his sister. "Robert could give you everything you want. You would ride in the finest automobiles and carriages and be respected as a doctor's wife. If you marry Ormond, the only thing you will hold is a subway strap in your hand."

"Why is this so important to you?"

"If Robert is not the man you want, I have several other friends who are doctors that I could introduce you to." He blatantly ignored her question.

"I'm hanging up now."

Henry heard a click as Mahala replaced the receiver in its cradle and the line went dead.

CHAPTER 43
Mahala

New York

MAHALA ASKED RUBY TO HELP her make the preparations for her wedding. It would be a small, simple gathering in May—neither of their families would be able to travel so far—and now that she knew Ormond was the one, Mahala didn't want to wait too long. As they ticked through Mahala's to-do list—getting fabric for a dress, reserving the church, flowers—Ruby shared her own wedding stories. They laughed and rolled their eyes, remembering the lengths Ruby's and Jerome's families had gone to in trying to pair them off.

"I really admire you for sticking to your principles." Ruby smiled at her. "You didn't bow to your parents' pressure back then or Henry's pressure now. I couldn't have done that," she admitted.

Mahala set down her notes and gave Ruby a hug. She thought of when they were just two young girls playing in the surf finding shells. "Strength comes in different forms. You were there for me when I needed you most. You're like a sister to me. I couldn't have done this without you."

Mahala accompanied Ormond to his church for a meeting with the priest who would marry them. Father Bernardi was dressed in his typical attire of black suit, black shirt, and white collar when he answered the door to his office in the rectory. He motioned the couple in and directed them to have a seat in the two chairs in front of his large wooden desk. He walked around the desk and took a seat himself.

"I just have a few questions for you. They are more of a formality, but nonetheless I must ask." Ormond and Mahala nodded.

"You both are free to marry? You consent to this union? You intend to marry for life and be open to children?" He rattled the words off like one long question.

"Yes," they said in unison.

"Good. There's just one more matter." He looked at Ormond and flicked his eyes back to Mahala. "Ormond tells me that you are not Roman Catholic, is that right?" Father Bernardi probed.

"No, Father, I'm Episcopalian," Mahala answered.

"You are baptized, though, right?"

"Yes, of course."

He scribbled something in his note pad. "I'll need proof of your baptismal certificate."

Mahala began to feel the color rise in her cheeks.

"Can I get your promise that any future children resulting from this marriage will be brought up in the Catholic faith?" He looked at Ormond.

"Yes," Ormond answered.

Mahala knew that it was important to Ormond to be married in his church, so she was pleasant with the priest and nodded her assent.

"Marriage is a holy sacrament between Catholics. If you're not both Catholic, you'll need official permission from the diocese, which I will recommend since you're a baptized Christian." He glanced at Mahala. "However, there are some limitations that you should be aware of."

Ormond reached over to hold Mahala's hand and gently squeezed it. She resisted the urge to remove his hand from hers. Her eyes began to narrow as she listened to this pompous man speak about his *limitations*.

"Even with permission from the diocese, I'm afraid I can't allow the ceremony to be held on the altar. It will have to be beyond the step of the sanctuary."

"Catholics certainly have a lot of very important rules." Mahala smiled to lighten the sarcasm she intended. She could tell by the way Father Bernardi's face dropped that he received her meaning.

At the end of the meeting, Ormond stood up and shook Father Bernardi's hand. They walked out of the church office, Ormond's gentle hand placed on Mahala's back.

"May, I know it's frustrating to deal with all these rules. I'm sorry if he offended you."

"He's not the most flexible man in the world now, is he?" She tried to make light of the situation.

"I'm marrying the woman I love, and I don't care how I have to do it as long as I can do it."

He pecked her on the cheek, and she softened. She was hopelessly in love with this man.

"I'll let the church win this one, but only because I want to be your wife."

Mahala chose an elegant two-piece dress for her wedding and made the alterations herself. She created a small pouch in the seam of the upper half of the dress, where she stitched in the tiger cowrie shell that she and Ruby now always exchanged at momentous events in their lives.

Ormond wore an elegant tailored gray suit, altered by Mahala's own hands, and his best leather oxford shoes, which he had polished up at the shoemaker for the occasion. He was of modest means, but he knew how important it was to Mahala to be well dressed—and he wanted to make things up to her about not being allowed to marry at the altar.

They had a small celebration after exchanging their vows and spent their wedding night in the new apartment on Nagel Avenue in Inwood, which Ormond had rented as their new home.

The young couple wasted no time starting a family. In late August, as soon as Mahala realized she was pregnant, she started to plan how best to inform Mr. Koifman. She figured she had until at least Thanksgiving before she would begin to show, especially if she let out the waistband on her skirts and make sure to wear a jacket to hide any growing bump.

She was conflicted about leaving the workforce and starting a family. She liked the independence that working afforded her, but she did want to have a child—and to stay home and raise him or her, at least in the beginning. This, in its own way, was also something that she could *choose*; she was still in control of her own destiny.

When she finally told Mr. Koifman, he was not happy to be losing her, but he had long ago accepted that this was what young women did once they became a wife. Mr. Koifman did not subscribe to the marriage bar policies of many other businesses, which automatically fired any woman who married in favor of a single woman who needed to work to support herself. Even at Koifman's, most of the young single girls quit as soon as they were married, not even waiting until they became pregnant. Mahala was the exception, working into her second trimester, giving the working floor gossips fresh fodder at her expense. Even Ormond tried to convince her to quit her job.

"May, don't you think that it's time to stay home? Tell Koifman that you're finished," he demanded.

Mahala inhaled slowly before she answered her husband. "I will quit my job to raise this baby, but I will do it in my time. Don't rush me," she warned.

"They will all think that I don't have a good enough job to support my family," he complained.

She tried not to roll her eyes. "You and I both know that's not so. I'm just working a little longer because I enjoy it, and it doesn't hurt that I'm putting some money away for expenses when the baby comes."

"It can't come soon enough as far as I'm concerned. I don't feel right about you waiting so long," he said, relenting.

∞

They were blessed with their first child the following May—a beautiful baby girl. By Mahala's estimation, she had already contributed so much physically to the child that she allowed her husband to choose her name. Ormond beamed when he held their perfect newborn, with her wavy ebony hair and smooth soft skin, in his arms. "Wilma," he said softly. Mahala agreed it was perfect.

Mahala refused to be separated from her baby for even the shortest period of time and took her not only to doctor's visits but to the market, the butcher shop, the bakery, and everywhere around the whole of Inwood. She strolled over to Ruby's at least once a week to visit with her and her baby. Her pram already had so much mileage on it that Ormond had to change the wheels. Mahala was not in a rush to get back to Koifman's. She dedicated herself to motherhood and was finding it very enjoyable and rewarding to care for this little baby girl—and a good thing, too, because the couple found themselves pregnant again quickly. Wilma was just over one year old when Mahala was about to give birth to her second child in the summer.

This time, Ormond approached her with a surprising request, grabbing a slice of toast as he prepared to leave for work. "Mahala, let's have this one in St. Vincent."

She looked at him agape, still queasy with morning sickness that hardly limited itself to mornings only. Wilma wobbled over, grabbing her skirt to be picked up.

"We can have the support of our extended family there. There will be many sleepless nights for you when the baby comes, and you will be too exhausted to look after Wilma in the way you've become accustomed to," Ormond pleaded. "My sister can come and be a tremendous help, and your nieces are old enough to babysit for Wilma. Won't you please consider it?"

She shook her head. "We're just beginning to make a life here in New York, Ormond. I don't want to go running home when things get hard. We belong here with each other and our growing family. I also have Ruby *here* and we always help each other out with the children."

"Don't you want Jane and Kavita to see their grandchildren? It's much harder for them to travel than it is for us. If we don't go to St. Vincent, who knows when they will see the new baby, or even Wilma for that matter? If we do this, then they can spend an extended period of time with the children, and we can return to New York when we are ready." Something about his voice sounded off to her.

"That's not the real reason why you want to go, is it?" Mahala raised one eyebrow as she shifted Wilma from one hip to the other. "It's not just to get me the help you think I need. You have some ulterior motive," she stated.

"N-no," he stammered. "Well, maybe you're right . . . I want this baby to be born in the British West Indies. We had Wilma in New York, and she's already such a city child—I want her to be connected to our island home. With this second baby, if he or she is born in St. Vincent, they will have a visceral connection to our island home and our beginning," Ormond implored, his eyes bright.

"Let me think about it," she replied as she set the baby down and led her out of the room, holding her hand.

When the time came, Mahala decided to appease her husband. With Wilma in tow, they traveled to St. Vincent, where Kavita welcomed them back into her home. Mahala soon gave birth to a son, named Ormond after his father.

Mahala encouraged her husband to accept temporary work with his old buddies who were house builders on Bequia. It would be easy for him to hop on the daily ferry service between the islands. Her goal was to keep them from depleting their savings. Equally as important, she thought, was the fact that he would not be idle. He needed to work with his hands, to stay busy, or he'd drive himself—and her—crazy. Ormond's sister Marion brought a continuous supply of meals for them, which they thoroughly appreciated. The two grandmothers cooked their signature dishes and kept everyone's stomachs sufficiently full. Mahala soaked up all the attention she and her newborn son received. She felt loved and cared for in a way she hadn't felt since she was a small child herself.

CHAPTER 44

Jane

St. Vincent, British West Indies

JANE CAUGHT A GLIMPSE OF Sofia and Lily wheeling Wilma back and forth in front of the house. Sofia pushed while Lily stuck by her side, picking up the small stuffed bear that Wilma continued to hurl out of the carriage. She could see Wilma waving her arms in delight every time Lily returned the bear to her. The bear's once-white fuzzy coat was now marred with splotches of dirt that resembled bruises. She would definitely need to wash that before Wilma took a nap with it.

Suddenly, Jane noticed dark clouds overhead. The trees swayed gently as the wind moved in over the water and up the side of the island. She poked her head out the door and waved to them. "Come on back inside, girls, before it starts to pour."

She met the trio at the door and plucked Wilma out of the carriage. "Oh my, what have we here?" Jane asked. "Is anyone hungry?" She headed for the kitchen.

"We're starved!" Sofia said, following Jane. "We just wanted to take Wilma for a ride so that Aunt Mahala could spend time with the new baby," she added proudly.

"That's very nice of you, sweetheart." Jane stroked Wilma's soft curls and placed her down in the highchair at the table. She reached up for the stack of little white plates with pink flowers that the girls loved so much. Then, using the dish towel she had tucked into her apron, she uncovered the cast iron pot on the stove top, laden with her signature curried chicken. The girls' eyes widened at the sight of the thick mustard-brown sauce. The aroma instantly filled the kitchen and made their mouths water with anticipation. Overhead, rain began to drum on the roof.

"Grandma, that smells so good," Sofia trilled.

Jane stuck a fork into a drumstick, and the meat pulled away from the bone. She placed it onto the first plate and ladled the rich curry sauce over the top. The sauce clung to the chicken and made a small pool below the exposed part of the bone. She turned to load the next plate and saw the trees outside had begun to bend and sway even more. The wind howled and whipped across the yard. Small debris swirled upward and blew away. The sky grew darker, and the wind intensified.

Jane dropped the plate back to the counter and ran to close the windows and shutters. This was a tropical storm. She had seen many over the years and knew the damage could be severe if there was a storm surge. Flooding and landslides were terrifyingly common, and this one had blown in fast and hard. Jane remembered the last extreme hurricane, back when John was alive. He had taken charge of securing their safety while she handled reassuring the children. She'd been so grateful then. This time, she was on her own.

She called to Sofia, "Secure the door! I'll get the rest of the windows." She looked over her shoulder to see Lily grabbing Wilma out of the highchair. "Get under the table and don't let her go for anything!" she barked. She was scared but she didn't want either of the girls to know. Stay there until I tell you to come out." Wilma wailed for her mother.

Within a half hour, the wind shook the walls so badly, Jane thought she could hear the corner of the roof start to lift up. Two bicycles scraped along the side of the house, pushed by the wind until they were clear of the wall and blown down the yard in a twisted pile of metal and rubber.

Rain came down in torrents and pounded against the shutters. Large streams gushed over the rocks and vegetation and carried dirt, debris, and small plants down toward the coastline. Water flowed from everywhere. It collected and rose in an enormous surge. The small plants and flowers on all sides of the house were soon completely submerged. Jane fought to keep the water from coming into the house but was only partially successful. Her efforts were no match for the storm.

A thick spidery flash of pure white ripped down from the black sky and struck the tallest palm tree in front of her house, searing straight through the wide trunk. It crashed down on the roof. Jane lurched away from the window where she'd been trying to shove more towels around the casement, retreating to the kitchen, where she crouched down and covered a sobbing Sofia. The roof creaked as it began to succumb to the weight and the strong gusts of wind. Jane assessed the risks in her head as she hugged her granddaughter closer to her body. The safety of the girls was her first priority. Kavita's house wasn't far, but in this raging storm . . . She prayed Mahala and the baby were safe.

Just then the door flew open as if unhinged by the ferocious wind. A second later, she saw Ormond in the doorway. Sheets of rain pelted him in the face. He squinted in order to scan the room and spotted Wilma squeezed under the table with her cousin. He bolted over, scooped Wilma up, and tucked her under his jacket before his gaze found Jane shielding Sofia.

"Jane, girls, come with me. This roof is about to collapse!" He headed back toward the flapping door, stealing a glance over his shoulder to make certain Jane was able to move.

The distance between her home and Kavita's was short—Jane knew this—yet in the torrential rain, water up to their ankles, it felt like a vast expanse. Jane held each granddaughter by the shoulders and followed her son-in-law. It was difficult to see through the violent rain whipping into her face, but she caught sight of Mahala running toward them. They all hurried inside Kavita's house.

Kavita was holding her grandson, a terrified look on her face. "I'm so relieved that you're okay. Mahala leaped out of her seat once she saw the tree smash down into your house! I was just praying she was going to make it without injuring herself."

Ormond, soaked to the bone, was now drenching the floor. "We both had the same instinct." He looked at his wife. "I saw the flash of lightening and then heard the enormous crash when I was just about here. I had to make sure that Jane and the girls were safe."

Mahala clung to Ormond with Wilma at his side. "Oh, my sweet, sweet baby dear. Let Mommy love you up." She grabbed her firstborn child and pulled her soaking body close to her. "Let's get you all out of these wet clothes," she said and looked over at Kavita. Kavita set the baby on his blanket, jumped into motion, and returned with towels and blankets piled high in her arms.

"That was too close." Mahala grabbed a towel and rubbed Wilma dry.

"Wilma was wailing, and I could barely even hear it over the storm raging," Jane shuddered. "When Ormond burst through my door, well, I've never been happier to see him."

CHAPTER 45
Mahala

A FEW DAYS AFTER THE storm, Ormond recruited some men from the sugar mill to help him repair Jane's roof. He also helped Kavita clean up the damage her property had sustained—uprooted plants, broken branches that needed to be raked up and disposed of. Mahala was grateful to Ormond for having not only the skills but also the willingness to help her mothers.

Now, she glimpsed him walking around the side of the house, dragging several gardening tools in his hands. She quickly warmed up the stew she had made yesterday—a delicious lunch as a reward for all of his efforts.

"Smells great! I'm famished." Ormond walked in, washed his hands, and immediately sat down and devoured his wife's cooking.

"The kids are both fed and down for their naps, so if you don't mind, I'm going to go over to Mama's house for a while just to check on her," said Mahala.

"Let me know if there's anything else that needs to be repaired over there."

"Okay." She kissed Ormond on the cheek and dashed out the door to take advantage of the time she had while the kids were napping.

She strolled into her mother's house, where she found Jane sitting on the couch working some embroidery on her lap. Jane looked up and motioned to Mahala to join her on the couch.

"Are you okay, Mama?"

Jane had a far-off look in her eye. "It's times like this that I really miss your father."

"I know, I miss him too." She moved close to her mother and put her arm around her. Mahala remembered sitting exactly in this same spot when she was a little girl, cuddling up to Jane, trying to get as close as she could.

"Mama, there's something I've been meaning to ask you. I . . . I don't know how to begin, so I'm just going to say it."

Jane turned to face her daughter.

"Mama, I've heard versions of the story since I was little but . . . I don't think I really understood how you and Papa could have done what you did."

Jane's fingers stilled. "Sweetheart, that was all so long ago."

"I know," Mahala said slowly, "but now that I'm a mother myself, I just can't ever imagine giving my child up to someone else. I would give my very life for my children. Why couldn't you make a sacrifice for me? To keep me, I mean?"

"You had a much more comfortable life than you could have had with us."

"I don't buy that. We've been living with this arrangement all these years and I love both my families, but can you understand how much it hurt to see all my brothers and sisters over here without me? And know that you willingly gave me up?" Tears sprang to her eyes.

"Kavita was devastated that she couldn't have a child of her own."

"That's not a reason to give *your* child away."

"It wasn't just that. We felt—we felt like we were in a vise. We were already having trouble putting food on the table, and your father made a catastrophic error at the mill which set us back even farther." She paused. Mahala stayed silent. "We thought about what Kavita had asked—she'd had this idea, you see, and when she asked, she knew she was asking for a sacrifice, a miracle—and we saw a way to change Ganesh and Kavi's lives that also offered us a path forward, one in which we wouldn't ever truly lose you."

"I'm not trying to take anything away from what I had with Mai and Dai," Mahala said, her voice cracking, "I just feel like I lost something. Can you understand that?"

"Oh, sweetheart, I never meant to hurt you." Tears flowed from Jane's eyes. "I love you so much, you have to know that."

"I do. I just wanted to understand why you did it. They had more traditional Indian values than you and Papa, and I paid that price. Honestly, how could you let them try to give me away at thirteen years old? Why didn't you object?"

"We thought it was a bit too early, but they felt that it was the right decision. They wanted to secure a future for you."

"That's what I'm talking about. You didn't rush Betty into getting married at thirteen, and things turned out fine for her. When I look back on it now, I remember how alone I felt. I could have used your support."

Jane was silent for a moment. "I'm sorry. I don't know what else to say. I tried to do the best I could." She wiped her eyes of the tears streaming down her face. "I had no idea this was how you felt."

"I didn't feel the full impact of it either until I became a mother," said Mahala. She wrapped her arms around her mother. They sat together for a long time.

Epilogue

MAHALA AND ORMOND RETURNED TO New York with their two children, quickly adding a third to their family. She once again allowed Ormond to select the name—Erwin, to honor his best friend, a close army buddy whom Mahala had never been able to meet. She dedicated herself to raising her children while Ormond earned a living for them all.

Eventually, as the nation plunged into economic crisis, Ormond's company struggled to pay its expenses and experienced a severe slowdown in orders. He was fortunate to keep his job but was forced to accept a reduction in his salary.

As she worried over their latest rent bill, Mahala realized that if she returned to the workforce, she could increase the money she needed to run the house. She was getting the urge to get back to work anyway. She missed the sense of accomplishment that tailoring gave her, as well as the comradery of her coworkers.

The next evening, when Ormond walked through the door, he was rewarded with the rich unmistakable aroma of pot roast. Mahala always used her considerable culinary skills to elevate the flavor of the meal, no matter how limited the choices in the pantry. Her favorite trick for a rich dark gravy was to first caramelize the onions in her heavy-duty aluminum pot before browning the meat on top. The result was a tender roast with rich dark gravy.

Mahala spotted Ormond through the cloud of aromatic steam escaping the pot. She had been tending the roast for three hours already and timed it perfectly for her husband's arrival.

"Hi, sweetheart," Ormond said, beaming. He kissed his wife on the cheek. "That smells wonderful!" He reached into the icebox and pulled out a bottle of beer.

"You'll spoil your supper. Put that back for later," Mahala playfully scolded her husband. Ormond returned the bottle and gently closed the icebox door.

"How long until supper is ready? I'm ravenous!"

"Just a few minutes now. I'll feed the children first, then you and I can sit down. You have a little time to unwind." She handed him his newspaper.

Ormond tucked it under his arm and headed toward his reading chair sans beer.

After dinner—the children first, then the adults—Mahala pushed back from the table, took her plate and reached for Ormond's, and headed over to the sink.

"I'm going back to work," she stated as a matter of fact.

He looked up, startled. "What do you mean? We're doing fine. You're the most economical housewife in Inwood."

"We could be doing better," she answered.

"You mean I could be doing better."

She turned and raised an eyebrow at him. "We need more income. The boys are growing, and that's not going to stop anytime soon. Erwin can wear Ormond's hand-me-downs, but Ormond needs new clothes and shoes and so does Wilma. I do the best I can, but if I went back to work, money wouldn't be so tight anymore."

"You just have to do a better job of budgeting and making my paycheck stretch for our needs."

"You just said that I was the most economical housewife," she almost shouted, but thought of the kids in the next room. "I can't make money out of thin air, but I can make money if I go back to work." She dropped the dishes in the sink with a clatter.

"You should be home taking care of the children and the house and me. *That's* your job. The neighbors will talk. They'll think I can't support my family," Ormond bellowed.

"We can't control what the neighbors think, but we can control our own destiny. I'm not asking for permission." With that, she turned on her heel and strode out of the room.

The next morning, Ormond rose and silently left the house without a word to Mahala. He was still fuming from their fight the night before, she could tell. He had used the silent treatment tactic before. He didn't know what he was in for if he thought this was going to work on her.

She truly was not trying to insult his manhood. If Ormond's anger was the price she had to pay to provide for her family, so be it.

Five days of silence between them finally ended when Ormond broke.

"May, please . . . Why aren't you talking to me? We're like two strangers. I can't take it any longer."

"Me? *You're* the one who stopped talking to me. Don't you remember?"

"Let's not do this anymore. I don't want to fight . . . I—I know you're right. That's what really hurts me," Ormond admitted.

"I know." She stepped closer and wrapped her arms around her husband. "I love you and this family more than anything else in the world. You are everything to me. I'm so happy and proud of what we've created. I have the ability to make things a little easier on us. Don't you want our children to be better off than we were?" Mahala said with love in her voice. She let her words hang quietly between them. When he leaned back and turned to kiss her, she knew that she had won.

Mahala was an avid reader of fashion magazines. Her favorite was *Harper's Bazaar*. She loved the beautiful photographs of the glamorous models used to display high fashion and haute couture and imagined being able to create the gorgeous dresses that looked more like a work of art than clothing.

After years of flipping through the pages of chic hairstyles on all the models, she thought that now, while she was returning to work, was the perfect time to cut her luxuriously thick mane into a sophisticated coiffed bob. When she announced her intention to Ormond, he was vehemently opposed.

"You have the most beautiful hair. Why would you ever want to slash it off?"

"I don't want to *slash* it off. I'll go to the beauty parlor and get a bob. It's been the trend for several years. Besides, I need a change," Mahala explained as she lifted the lid of the simmering pot on the stove and began to stir its contents.

"Mahala, I don't want you to cut your hair," Ormond stated emphatically.

"It will be very stylish. You'll see. You'll like it," she offered.

"I won't like it. And not only that, I forbid you to cut it!" Ormond thundered.

Mahala pulled the spoon out of the pot, gave it one bang on the rim, and set it gently down on the spoon rest alongside of the stove. She did not acknowledge Ormond's edict.

She rose the next morning, got the children ready for school, and saw her husband off to work. She accepted his soft kiss on her cheek and handed him his lunch that she had prepared. She gently closed the door after his departure. She walked into her bedroom and sat at her makeup vanity. She carefully plaited her long hair into a single thick braid and powdered her face, returning the gold and white cover to the round box and placing the powder puff on top, satin side up. She headed out for her appointment.

Just past six, she heard the front door open and the sound of Ormond's keys being dropped on the hallway table by the door. She could picture him removing his hat and placing it on the coat rack. Then he entered the living room to greet his family, loosening his tie with one hand while holding a folded newspaper in the other. Wilma ran to him, giving him a kiss on the cheek, while Ormond and Erwin waved from the floor, too involved in a game of trains to formally greet their father.

"Daddy, do you want to look at my drawings? I just finished them!" Wilma said. She flipped her sketchbook to the first page.

"Sure, sweetheart, let me just hang up my jacket and take off my shoes." He shrugged out of his suit jacket. Mahala waited for him to notice.

"Sit next to me on the sofa, Daddy. I'll show you my work." Wilma slid closer to Mahala, making room.

Ormond leaned down to kiss Mahala and ruffle the boys' hair, then took a seat next to his daughter. It escaped him at first, but now, as he took in the view up close, she watched his face change as he realized that she had cut her hair. It just grazed the bottom of her earlobes and was blunt cut all the way around the back of her head. Parted on the right, it swept over in a subtle wave framing the left side of her face. She looked beautiful, but Ormond was horrified.

"May, your hair! What did you do? I expressly forbid you to cut it, and you went against my word and did it!" he shouted. His eyes were wide with disbelief. All three children exited the room quickly, leaving their books and trains.

"I told you I was going to do it. You can't really be that surprised," she said.

Ormond's mouth gaped open.

Mahala was happy with her life and her family in Inwood. She had a husband whom she loved, who loved her back, and three beautiful healthy children she adored. She wasn't rich, but she was far from the state of poverty that her brother had warned her of if she didn't marry someone of his choosing. She knew that she made the right choices for herself, even if they required sacrifice.

She made it a priority to stay in touch with her extended family, despite the fact that they lived in different countries. She even repaired her relationship with Henry, settling into a friendly rapport, trading visits between New York and Panama. In later years, Mahala was happy to welcome his sons at her house any time they were able to visit from Columbia, just a short subway ride away.

Mahala and Ormond and Ruby and Jerome invited each other for dinner at their respective homes often. All four friends still frequented the Portuguese Club on Saturday night when they could. Their children got along exceptionally well and became regular playmates. Mahala was gratified that her longstanding friendship with Ruby had created a new connection with the next generation.

She kept her passport up to date and well used. When air travel became more accessible, she was able to get around much faster than by ship and stay longer with her loved ones in St. Vincent, Barbados, Panama, and even Holland. She had a nephew in the Netherlands whom she made a point of visiting occasionally despite Henry's disapproval. Henry had attempted to hide the result of yet another of his dalliances by keeping the child far from his perfect life in Panama, but Mahala refused to be deterred. Blood was blood as far as she was concerned.

She made quite a reputation for herself in the Garment District as an expert tailor and a worker's advocate. She continued to work side by side with Ruby, both women able to hone their skills. She didn't take any mistreatment from anyone, especially not from her bosses.

When she thought about her life, her choices, the obstacles she faced—she was proud of herself for having the strength to follow her own path and make a life on her own terms. She was eternally grateful to Ruby for the incredible support she offered at a momentous time in her life.

Author's Note

THE CHARACTER OF MAHALA IS based on a real woman who grew up on St. Vincent in the early 1900s. Her name was Mahala Simons, and she was my paternal grandmother.

Her parents, Jane and John Simons, traveled to St. Vincent from Lucknow, India, in 1880 via ship along with over two hundred other East Indians to work as indentured servants on the small Caribbean island. They changed their Indian names in favor of more British-sounding names in their new home in the British West Indies. After their indenture was completed, they remained in St. Vincent for the rest of their lives.

Mahala was indeed adopted by her mother's best friend and neighbor, who was unable to conceive a child of her own. My great-grandmother never thought she would bear another child at the time. However, this was a promise she made out of love for her friend and upheld out of honor once she found out she was pregnant again.

My grandmother Mahala often told me the story of her unique upbringing. She enjoyed the benefits of being an only child in a family that was financially better off than her biological family. However, because of the open approach they took to her adoption, she was able to grow up with her biological siblings and parents right next door.

Many of the events in this novel are based on her actual life. She rejected the arranged marriage her family had planned for her as a young teenager. She had a sly smile on her face and a twinkle in her eye when she recounted this broken engagement story to me when she was in her early eighties. She really did spit in his eye!

In a patriarchal society and home, she did things her way, despite convention and the risk of personal peril. She cut her long hair off in the 1920s when it was fashionable to do so, despite her husband's objections. The fact that he forbade her was more reason for her to feel compelled to do it. She even kept the long thick black braid in her drawer. I remember her showing it to me when I was a kid playing in her apartment in New York.

She did leave the island of St. Vincent at the age of twenty-one to escape the pressure of her family trying to control her life. I was so proud of her for the courage and determination she showed at such an early age. She lived the rest of her life in New York, where she married my grandfather, Ormond Marks, and raised three children in the Depression era. My aunt Wilma convinced the family to legally change their surname back to the original Portuguese spelling of Marques. My father, Erwin, was her last child, born in 1929. She did go back to work in the Garment District as a tailor to help support the family when my father was in school, and my grandfather didn't talk to her for a week because of it, feeling as though his manhood were threatened by the simple act of his wife returning to the workforce. Of course, at that time, it was highly unusual for a woman to work outside of the home once she had children.

Born at the turn of the century in 1900, she was a strong, independent, intelligent, and outspoken women well ahead of her time. She was a true maverick and the beloved matriarch of our family.

The immense love I have for my grandmother compelled me to write this novel about her remarkable life. The process of writing it has been personally enlightening as I researched not only the events of her life, but also immersed myself in the events of that time period. I pored through boxes of old black-and-white photographs that curled at the edges, leafing through many family photo albums. I surrounded myself with those pictures and artifacts of her life as I wrote. To this day, I still can't walk by Coty face powder without stealing a whiff from the artfully decorated orange and gold canister. Every time I do, it brings back the scent of her for me.

I am forever grateful to her for sharing with me the details of her extraordinary life. I cherish the time we were able to spend together in those nineteen short years. When she came to visit, we would often sit at the kitchen table and talk for hours. I never tired of hearing the stories she was willing to tell me. My only regret is that I did not have the chance to delve deeper to answer some of the questions I have now. My father, Erwin, embodied much of my grandmother's characteristics and certainly inherited her gift of gab. We too often found ourselves at that very same kitchen table, talking the hours away. Sadly, my father passed away in 2014 at the age of eighty-five, and I was unable to share with him my tribute to his amazing mother. He knows how amazing she was because he lived with her.

In my research for this novel, I was able to connect with some cousins of mine on my grandmother's side that I never knew existed. I was also able to uncover the ship manifests for many voyages that my grandmother took to visit her extended family in St. Vincent and Panama.

In April 2024, almost one hundred years after my grandmother had left St. Vincent, I visited the island where she was born. I was able to experience the natural beauty of this lush volcanic island, from the rocky shores of the Windward Coast to the stunning waterfalls and sole volcano on the Leeward Coast. I made a trip to the National Archives and found the ship's manifest for the *Lightning*, which carried my great-grandparents to St. Vincent in 1880. I had the opportunity to take a ferry ride over to Bequia and connect with distant cousins of my grandfather, Ormond.

This is a work of historical fiction based on real people and events. I have changed some of the people's names, but for myself and my family, I have kept most names as they were. My real great-grandparents were Jane and John Simons. Mahala's adoptive parents' surname was Patandine; however, I changed their first names. Her siblings were Rudolph, Henry, Emily, and Elizabeth. Her best friend and sponsor when she came to New York was Ruby Govia. My grandmother worked for many harsh employers; Boris Koifman is an amalgamation of those individuals. I recently found out from my own mother that my grandmother again returned to work for a few short months in her late sixties in order to be eligible for a full pension. My grandfather, at that time in his life, could not be left alone all day. Consequently, he moved in with us temporarily so she could go to work and claim what was rightfully hers. I had no memory of this since I was a very small child at the time, but I smile when I think of it, knowing that such a headstrong, stubborn move to do things her way was truly classic Mahala.